# G R JORDAN

# Busman's Holiday

## *A Kirsten Stewart Thriller #9*

There's always that one summer that changes you

Beth Merlin, *One S'more Summer*

# Contents

# Foreword

This novel although set in Zakynthos, is entirely fictional and all persons, organisations and institutions conduct themselves in an entirely fictional fashion.

# Acknowledgement

To Ken, Jessica, Jean, Colin, John and Rosemary for your work in bringing this novel to completion, your time and effort is deeply appreciated.

# Novels by G R Jordan

Kirsten Stewart Thrillers (Thriller)

1. A Shot at Democracy
2. The Hunted Child
3. The Express Wishes of Mr MacIver
4. The Nationalist Express
5. The Hunt for 'Red Anna'
6. The Execution of Celebrity
7. The Man Everyone Wanted
8. Busman's Holiday
9. A Personal Favour


The Contessa Munroe Mysteries (Cozy Mystery)

1. Corpse Reviver
2. Frostbite
3. Cobra's Fang


The Patrick Smythe Series (Crime)

1. The Disappearance of Russell Hadleigh
2. The Graves of Calgary Bay
3. The Fairy Pools Gathering


Austerley & Kirkgordon Series (Fantasy)

1. Crescendo!
2. The Darkness at Dillingham

3. Dagon's Revenge
4. Ship of Doom


Supernatural and Elder Threat Assessment Agency (SETAA) Series (Fantasy)

1. Scarlett O'Meara: Beastmaster


Island Adventures Series (Cosy Fantasy Adventure)

1. Surface Tensions


Dark Wen Series (Horror Fantasy)

1. The Blasphemous Welcome
2. The Demon's Chalice

# Chapter 01

Kirsten Stewart looked at the long, cool, blue sea in front of her drifting off to the horizon and thought that she might stand up and take a walk out to it. It wasn't like the Scottish seas, cold any time of year; instead, it was pleasant to go into and she could stay in it for hours. She'd already enjoyed a good swim that morning, and now she was soaking up the rays on this little hideaway of a Greek island.

In truth, it wasn't a hideaway, it was one of the larger islands—Zante, or Zakynthos as it was known in the mother tongue, but whatever you called it, it was paradise. Kirsten could feel the sun beating down upon her back and that normally would have caused her concern for she tanned rather quickly, but at this point in time, someone was plastering sun lotion across her back and down her legs. He had said to her that once he was finished, she was going to have to turn over so he could do her front and she had given him a cheeky quip, 'Not in public.'

Life was good. She had Craig, she had the sun, she had a chilled existence over these last two months and there hadn't been a hint of anyone from the service. They had simply cast her off, let her depart, and Craig with her.

Kirsten grinned; life was certainly good, and she'd grown closer to the man who was now rubbing her back. There were several little local restaurants where they would dine at night and then take a walk along the beach where she snuggled in his arms while they talked about everything and nothing. The nothing moments were relaxed but the everything moments at times were tense, for she'd had a lot to get off her chest; he, too. You didn't work in the service without picking up the baggage.

Kirsten thought the talking had done her better than any number of counsellors and they'd grown together spiritually, she thought, as well as just physically. The only guilt she felt was being away from the Scotland that she loved so well. She had friends there, friends she'd been through a lot with, some of which she doubted she'd see again. Dominic and Carrie-Anne had left the service, gone off together to somewhere like this, Kirsten hoped, but with what they'd done in their time in the service, they would keep a low profile. Sure, she had their numbers; she could always contact them, always reach them, but why? The last thing you did was go near somebody else from the service once they were out; just let them be.

Along from Kirsten was a man in a suit with a number of followers also dressed rather neatly. A small crowd was around him, locals mainly, but none of them wore beach clothing. There were, however, loose shirts as if they weren't at work, but rather there for a special event, small as it was. The man was making a speech. Kirsten's Greek wasn't particularly good, but he was talking about sewage.

At that point, she switched off. It was one of the reasons why she was lying face down. With nothing on top, she didn't want to be caught in some local paper, for there were a few cameras around this man. Part of her was hoping they'd leave, for until they had arrived, Craig and she had enjoyed the beach to themselves. True, there now seemed to be a family at the far end of the beach, but at least they had the decency to be running around in shorts.

Kirsten reached her right hand out to grab a bottle of water and found that she'd already drunk it.

'Have we got any more?' she asked Craig, behind her.

'No, you drank it. You know what you're like in this heat.'

'I know,' said Kirsten, 'and I'm feeling it, too.'

'Do you want me to go and get you another one? There's a shop just up from the beach; they'll have something.'

'No, I'll go. I'm absolutely boiling here. Do me good to stretch the legs. You lie down; you've been working hard enough on my back.'

'Well, it was a pleasure,' said Craig, smiling. Kirsten rolled to one side, then sat up, making sure her back was to the entourage close by. Craig handed her, first, her bikini top, and then, her t-shirt. She picked up a small purse from out of the bag beside her towel. 'I'll only be five minutes,' she said, and reached over and kissed him on the lips.

She stood up, walked away, and cast a couple of glances back. Each time, he was watching, but she didn't care. This had almost become their private beach, nearly as good as the flat. She'd manage with the intrusion today, and she didn't think anything could break the way she felt.

Kirsten took the fifty steps back up to the roadside and then walked along, staring at the smooth surface and dusty sides of the road that she was amazed looked so well in the baked heat. Back home with the snow and the ice, potholes were always forming here and there, and roadworks were just part of life.

Here, the roads of Zakynthos seemed to be in reasonably good nick for the mopeds that raced around the island, hired by tourists. That's what you saw in this part of the island, for they were far away from the main town of Zante. Craig and she had also kept away from a lot of the other holiday traffic where the tourist industry flew in throughout the summer. Instead, they'd found a local flat in a small village, and Kirsten decided it was paradise.

Having bought her water, she walked back along the road, still in her bare feet. She looked out to sea where there was a large yacht passing by. Kirsten wondered if they could go there next. Imagine being out on the sea for several weeks and no one else. Solitude seemed good, as long as it was solitude with Craig.

When reaching the top of the steps, Kirsten could hear a commotion on the beach below. Looking down, she saw people running here and there, and she quickly tried to locate Craig, over by her towel. She saw no one. She clocked her bag was still there, his towel beside hers, but nowhere was Craig to be seen. There was a crowd, a smaller number than before, gathered around something in the sand.

Kirsten decided not to rush there, but walked down, giving the impression of just an interested on-looker wondering what was happening. Her heart was beginning to thump, Craig wasn't there. If he'd split, run away because of something, he'd have come towards her, especially if he thought it wasn't anything to do with him, maybe instead just something that they didn't want to get caught up in.

As she got closer, she could pick out various words spoken by the locals. There was the mention of blood, mention of a mayor, something about kidnapping, people taken in cars, racing off on the road. Kirsten pushed her way into the gathered crowd and saw a body on the sand. It was the man in the suit, the one who had been speaking earlier. She could see the blood drenching through his shirt and every sinew within her tensed.

She glanced around. Craig was nowhere, nowhere. Quickly she walked over to where their towels lay in the sand. On reaching, she saw Craig's had blood on it, it wasn't a large amount, certainly by no standard of the mayor's only thirty feet away. Kirsten reached down to the bag. Craig's wallet was still there, and around the edges of the bag she dived into a small pocket and found Craig's gun.

It had taken them time when they had arrived to organise themselves, to set up the flat and their belongings how they wanted. Neither of them was daft enough to think that being out of the service meant that nobody would ever come after them again. Safety was always on their mind, but if Craig reacted to an incident, he mustn't have thought it was dangerous or the gun would have gone with him. Her own gun was also in the bag. She slung the bag over her shoulder. Quickly she wrapped up the towels, pushing them away inside the bag as well.

As Kirsten turned to walk towards the steps, she saw the police arriving and decided she needed to bypass them. Slowly, she walked along the beach until she got to the far end where she joined a small path leading up to the road. More and more police were arriving and what looked like ambulances as well. She walked along the road back towards the steps that led down as if she'd just arrived and grabbed the local who was standing there. She asked him what was happening, and his reply was a blur.

He fired off a statement she could barely hang on to, a mayor had been knifed and was dead but other people had been taken, other people had disappeared, one man in particular. Kirsten's stomach went tight. Craig had been taken? Was Craig gone? Why was Craig gone?

Kirsten had no information, so she wandered along close to the police cars. As she arrived, a policeman stepped in front of her, and she feigned ignorance, not speaking any Greek.

'I don't understand what's happening? Can you tell me what's happening?'

'You can't go, you can't go to the beach. Beach off limits. You need to go to another beach.'

'Why, but why are you all here? This is a nice beach,' she said, 'I was going to go here because they said it was a really good beach to swim in.'

'No, you can't come here. No go here,' said the man. 'Person dead, someone has died. We need to work.'

'Someone's dead?' asked Kirsten, feeling surprised.

'Yes, and someone taken, someone we think British.

'Are people after British people . . . because I'm British?'

'Were you meeting someone?' asked the man.

'No,' said Kirsten. It was the truth, just not the whole truth. 'Who was taken?'

'British man. They say he tried to help then he was kidnapped.'

'Kidnapped where?'

'We don't know. Please, please go back. Go to another beach, not this beach, okay? You help me, you go.'

The man's English was not great but was probably better than Kirsten's Greek. She turned as asked and started walking back down the road towards the village. She gave the air that she was a little confused, but otherwise, she was returning back to the rest of her day, but inside, everything hurt, her stomach was hollow. They'd got Craig. They'd grabbed Craig. Why?

Kirsten walked away from the police officer, but once she was round the corner, she sat down just off the roadside under a small tree. The shade wasn't particularly cooling, and she wished it had been. For a while, she was trying to think about what best to do. She could feel the sweat pouring down her face.

If somebody had come for him, why here? Why now? The police officer said that Craig had reacted, gone to help, been involved that way. It made sense; he wouldn't have grabbed the knife if he thought somebody was just hassling someone. Even when they'd taken out the knife, Craig would probably bank on himself being able to handle it with just his hands, not draw a weapon that he wasn't meant to have. Too easy to walk into a local feud.

The very least Kirsten was going to have to do was get changed. She was in a bikini with a t-shirt that was clinging to her from the sweat that was pouring off her in the cauldron of the midday sun. The best option was to return to the flat, pick up her gear and work out how to track down Craig. If they were talking about him being British, maybe he was being taken hostage for a reason. God help them if they had him hostage. She'd go and get him back and they'd better not stand in her way.

Kirsten stood up, flung the bag over her shoulder again, and began to walk into the village. She took the bottle of water out from her bag trying not to curse as she opened the top and drank the water. If only she'd been there, maybe together they'd have handled it better, maybe together.

You couldn't second guess yourself. This might just be a minor incident. Yes, the mayor was dead, but maybe Craig was just something extra. Somebody to make money out of. It certainly didn't look like anybody from the past was coming for them. After all, this wasn't the place to do it and they would've taken Kirsten as well. She looked at her watch, maybe half an hour Craig had been gone. Time to get to the flat, get changed, get on the trail before it went too cold.

# Chapter 02

Kirsten found herself breathing in a staccato motion as thoughts spun in her head. She was trying to follow her practice of remaining cool, calm, thinking through what was going on, and trying to pick out the best plan of action, but this was Craig. This was the man she had shared her bed with for the last two months. This was the man she was thinking about sharing her life with.

As she walked through town, she tried to focus, concentrating on looking at the faces she walked by. There was the man from the bread makers, a local she'd always seen. He smiled over at her. That was pretty normal, for he liked her. Every time she went into the bread shop he seemed to give her a little bit extra, whether it be another croissant in the bag or a bread roll. He was always kind to her, and now he was smiling over at her. She gave her grin back as best she could, but she felt like she was going to swoon, collapse from the weight of pressure piling down on top of her.

There was the woman who was always at the front of her little house, cleaning, sweeping who knew what into the street. She said good day to Kirsten, who fumbled with the word before saying it back. She crossed the dusty road and looked at their flat high up on the side of a bank. There were two other flats underneath but the outside steps ran up to reach theirs. The top floor flat had a good view of the road and from up there you could see everyone passing by.

It was also hard to get to; you'd have to come up the steep steps. Craig picked it for that reason, knowing anyone coming to get them in that flat would find it difficult, and most agencies wouldn't have bothered. They'd wait until they'd gone out. That gave Kirsten and Craig the chance to identify them watching the flat.

After assessing the flat from street level, she ran up the steps quickly, not because she wanted to but because that's what she always did. Craig always seemed to lumber up them after her and she would be first in the shower, or first to take over the sofa. When she'd stepped inside the house, sometimes she would wait behind the closed door until he opened it and then she'd welcome him into the house with a kiss. Just a daft thing that had started up these last two months, something that was very un-Kirsten.

On reaching the top of the steps, she unzipped her bag, reaching inside for a weapon. After setting the bag on the ground, she took her keys out with her other hand, opened the door and slowly pushed it back. She stepped in almost nonchalantly or at least that's the way it looked. There was a fear running in the back of her mind, but it was keeping her senses keen because if she didn't think about what was going to happen, checking if someone was in the room, she'd have been thinking about Craig and all of her training would not be coming to the forefront.

Kirsten looked at the living room and saw that nothing was different. She closed the door behind her and locked it. She walked down the small corridor to the back bedroom. It was as they left it, the covers in a mess from their activities that morning. She'd had to practically drag him out to the beach because he'd wanted to stay there, but there was more than one way to have fun and Kirsten wanted her swim. Beside the bed was a photograph of the pair of them taken on that same beach less than a month ago.

Kirsten stepped out towards the kitchen which was a small affair where everything was in its place. There was only one more room and as Kirsten opened the door she saw the punch bag hanging from the ceiling, not moving. She called it her sweat room, because unlike back in Scotland, she sweated in here before she'd even begun her workout. The gloves were still in place, sitting over on the floor. The mats hadn't been moved, the weights, as always, in their corner as well.

They'd only arrived two months ago. The first month had been chaotic trying to find the flat, trying to get sorted, trying to work out where they would stash all their necessaries. Just because they were retired spies didn't mean that they could just give everything up. There were grab bags to be sorted. They'd look for locations around the island where they could drop gear, places to run to with enough money to get back out if they had to. Different passports obtained and ready for use.

They hadn't used their real names either, choosing Greg and Anne instead. Then there was the whole tale of how they'd run off to Gretna Green, but it had been closed because they got the wrong day. A whole back story that they'd practiced together. It would change one day, one day when they were happy enough but until then she was Anne Kirsten Campbell.

Kirsten sat down on her sofa thinking about what was next. First, she should get changed. She couldn't go after Craig wearing a bikini and a t-shirt. That was for sure. What would she do? What was the best way to go about this? The police were clearly onto something. Lots of information would flow through there. She'd need to get down to the local station and try and work out what had happened.

At some point, they'd realise it was Greg that had been taken, as Craig was known. The local people would ask; somebody may even have spotted him. Maybe even somebody would call around here. If it was simply a kidnapping of a British tourist, that wouldn't be a problem, but if it got out to the British authorities, they'd realise it was Craig. Others would get involved, just in case it wasn't. They would wonder if he was going to be handed back, and where had the woman gone who was with him?

Kirsten decided she would need to clean up, then get out and down to the police station to file Greg as missing and keep up the pretence of their new lifestyle. Otherwise, they could blow their cover. If she didn't bother, they'd ask why hadn't she come to them? It opened up too many questions. She also might get more information if she went down there. She'd just have to avoid that officer she'd spoken to. Already, things were getting sticky.

Kirsten stood up, turned, and looked out the window. She wasn't worried about anybody coming after her. After all, how many people really knew she was there? If they'd come for the mayor, they wouldn't have been looking for her.

She walked to the kitchen to get some cold water from the fridge and drank a glass of it before walking back and looking out of the large window at the front of their lounge. The street looked just as it usually did, an occasional person walking past, the car parked outside the barber's, the one the barber drove off in whenever a street warden came around because strictly, he shouldn't have parked it there. It was a comical event on a daily basis that always made Kirsten laugh except now, for there was a strange car beside it.

She stepped back from the window, moved along to one side and peered out from the corner of the window so she couldn't be seen. She watched for a moment. Someone stepped out of that car and was looking up towards her flat. He walked away down the street, then came back again and looked up. She watched as he gave a thumbs up for someone higher up from the street, someone that would have been outside her door. Kirsten dived from the window towards her kitchen as her door was battered open. She heard the wood splinter and a gunshot flew across the room.

She had left her own weapon back in the bedroom, having felt the premises were secure. Kirsten heard the footsteps of at least two people, and she grabbed a large kitchen knife from the block on the kitchen side bar. There was only one way into the kitchen but there was a breakfast bar and she ducked under it. The two men would have to swing in from the lounge through to the kitchen, and what they wouldn't see was the underside of the breakfast bar.

As she saw the feet step round, she leapt out from underneath the breakfast bar, catching the first one in the gut with her knife and throwing a punch into the face of the second one. As he fell backwards, she kept the knife driving up into the first man and ripped the gun from his hand. He fell to the ground clutching his stomach with the knife still in it, while Kirsten turned to the second man and unloaded the weapon into him. She spun around the corner of her kitchen to see two more men coming in the door and threw herself back to the kitchen as gunfire erupted. She heard the front window being shot out.

She kept herself down low in the kitchen, wondering if they'd move. There was no sign of movement from them, and she decided not to wait. Standing up, she went to the wall where there was a small hatch for serving through into the lounge. Quickly, but quietly, she undid the latch and threw it open catching the two men walking across the room. The first she tagged straight to the forehead; the second one managed to move out of the line of fire as Kirsten shot through.

She reckoned he'd peek into that hatch and fire through the first chance he had. If he did so, the kitchen being so small meant it'd be difficult to miss her, so Kirsten ran to the opening where she'd come in from the lounge. As she got to the corner and looked round, she saw the man at the hatch firing into the kitchen. She tagged him from where she was watching and saw him tumble to the floor.

The man who had been knifed in the gut was still moaning and Kirsten delivered a kick to his head to make sure he wouldn't speak again. She ran to the door and peered out to see a number of men running up the steps. There were cries from down on the street and Kirsten knew she'd have to get on the move quickly before the police arrived and closed it off. After all, they were only down the road, dealing with the mayor's murder.

She peered out of the door again, fired into the air, stopping those running up the steps for a moment. As they crouched down, worried they were going to be directly in the line of fire, she turned, ran to her sweat room where she punched open a cupboard and grabbed the bag inside. Running back, she again fired out through the open front door, hoping it would cause them to slow their ascent up the steps.

She made a quick visit into her bedroom to grab the guns that were in the bag before coming to the front door again. As she arrived, someone stepped in and she lashed a kick at his hand, which held a gun. The gun flew up to the air and Kirsten reached up grabbing the man's head and pulled it down into her knee. He fell to one side.

Another man stepped in behind him with a machine gun in his hand. Kirsten quickly grabbed him from the side, but he had started to fire the machine gun and it peppered the walls of the flat. Kirsten held his arms, forcing the machine gun up into the roof, for she knew nobody was above her. Anything into the floor might have injured someone in the flats below.

She drove him to the ground by kicking into the back of his knees and the machine gun spilled from his hands. She clocked him with a punch to the face, hopefully knocking him out cold, but she kicked the machine gun away to be on the safe side. She peered out and saw more people at the bottom of the steps and police cars starting to arrive.

Not hesitating, she jumped up onto the wall that surrounded the stairs that climbed up to her flat. From there, she saw the steep drop onto the hillside away from the steps. Kirsten leapt, cursing as she landed on some sharp twig causing her to yelp. She was still in her bare feet, still wearing what she had on at the beach, but aware that time was of the essence.

She could stay, try to explain to the police, but she didn't know them. She didn't know if they were on anyone's side. Were they corrupt or were they just good decent officers? She couldn't take the risk. People had come for her, but why? Had they simply identified that this is where the kidnapped man lived and come to make sure nobody else had seen them?

Whatever the case, she had left a few of them for the police.

Kirsten ran across the dusty hillside towards a vicious drop. It was steep enough so she couldn't run down it. She dropped onto her bottom and began to slide down it but felt the gravelly ground ripping up against her backside. As she reached the bottom, feeling somewhat bruised, she tore off along the street.

Two miles outside of town, in one of the coastal inlets, there was a cave. It was hard to see and went deep into the hillside. At the end of it would be enough rations, clothing, and money for her to begin her hunt for Craig. There would also be mobile phones to contact whoever she needed.

She stepped across the road, went off onto the hillside into a rich olive grove and began to run through it at speed. She needed to get to safety. She needed to get herself organised and then she needed to go find Craig.

# Chapter 03

Kirsten looked along the beach and made sure she walked up only on the rocks as she headed for the cave. It had a small opening but reached back deep into the rock and really had been quite a find. During their first couple of weeks, Craig and she had sought out potential hides, setting up four of them as they looked to settle down for three to four months at least.

*He had said a year*, thought Kirsten, *a year here doing nothing but just exploring the two of us.* Maybe they'd take up a small job. She'd always wanted to be a barista, making the coffee for the punters as they came along. She reckoned she got that from working with Macleod, the Detective Inspector she'd been under during her time with Police Scotland. He was always coffee this, coffee that, and she had learnt a lot from it, so much so that she had wanted to become a barista to see if she could actually put a passable coffee in front of him.

As she scanned the beach around her, she gave a smile. Those were good days, days when life seemed a lot simpler, days before he told her to go for a job with the service, a job that now seemed to have gone. The path she'd taken put her into a world of trauma and then she thought she was out of it as

Craig and she started a new life here in Zante or at least kicked about for a year.

When the beach was clear, Kirsten turned, sprinted up the rocks in her bare feet and climbed inside the cavity that led into the deeper parts of the rock. She had to slide past at one point and then crawled her way along in the dark until she found it on the floor, to her left a torch, a small rubber one with batteries, something that people might just leave behind.

Flicking it on, she saw where the cave swung off to the left, a place not to go down for there was a drop just after that, one that would be awkward to get back out of. However, to the right, the cave opened up to a point where things could be stored although she had to sit on her bottom to enter that gap. It was well out of the way, and she could light up the space knowing that no one could see it from the outside, even at night-time.

Kirsten saw the small waterproof bag sitting in the corner. She unzipped it, took out the lantern and switched it on. The batteries might last for five or six hours. She wouldn't be holing up inside the cave for that long, just long enough to get something to eat, settle down, and think what her next plan of attack would be.

Kirsten rummaged in the bag and found a tin of beans. There was a can opener as well. She made use of a small fork once the tin was open, to hungrily gulp the beans into her. She took the water from the grab bag, drank it, and then lay back. It was starting to get cold inside the cave. It was well sheltered from the sun's rays, so she reached into her grab bag, pulling on a fleece. She pulled her legs up inside it and sat huddled, thinking about what to do next.

Somebody had knifed the mayor and Craig had been

grabbed. It seemed Craig had gone to the rescue. He couldn't have thought it was that bad because he didn't take the gun with him. Somebody had driven off with him as well. Had they heard he was British and thought, *Let's make something else out of this situation?* It was strange if they were just going to assassinate someone. Assuming that's what the mayor's attack was.

On arrival in Zante, Craig and Kirsten had looked into the local underworld. She didn't think there were many terrorists that occupied the island although there were some significantly bad elements. There were drugs being run into some of the larger towns, but they weren't stupid either. This was a holiday destination. The money came in from tourists on their vacations. The last thing the local gangsters needed to do was make it somewhere that tourists didn't want to come, for their own people would rebel on them. That's how their living was earned.

There was however, within Greece, an unhappy contingent. People were not happy with how the economy was being run, how they'd had to go and beg to the European Union for assistance. People who were proud. She knew that even within Zante there'd been the occasional attack on the public services and on those who kept law and order. Most had been done out of holiday season and away from the main holiday areas, but it was there nonetheless. These people had never taken a hostage.

When Kirsten had worked in Scotland, she'd had sources to go to, people she could contact. She was also working for the agency who had their feelers here, there, and everywhere. People stationed within organisations undercover for years. Here she was in Zante with nothing but her own wit.

Her stomach growled despite the beans. She also felt sick to her core. She knew she had to act quickly, had to get on the move, but she didn't know where, how best to cover the island. People would now be looking for her. One key thing she'd have to do was keep a low profile.

She could do with somebody on the outside, she thought. Somebody looking at this situation, working the internet and searching into anybody she'd found that was attached to Craig in any way. She couldn't go to Anna and back to the service, not after what happened last time. They'd seen her as betraying them . . . a loose cannon.

There was no way Godfrey would sanction anything to do with Kirsten. She didn't want to, but she'd have to pick up a call to an old friend. Not Macleod. His life was very different, not tangled up in these darker things. No, she'd need to talk to her old team Dom and Carrie-Anne, wherever they were.

Kirsten placed a SIM card inside the phone that was located in the bag in the cave. She sent a text message through with eight individual digits. She no longer had a specific set of numbers that she could call Dom with. Instead, there was a code, one he would recognise so he would pick up the call when that number rang him. He would also know to be somewhere where no one could listen and make sure his phone call wasn't traced. Kirsten sent a text message and sat back waiting. She'd give him ten minutes. That would be enough for Dom to be somewhere else, somewhere private.

The silence was the worst bit. Kirsten wanted to put on the radio, something to keep away the thought of what could possibly be happening to Craig. She hoped he was with terrorists. She hoped he hadn't been picked up by someone else. She didn't think so. She didn't think that it was an old enemy, but in her game, you always had to entertain the possibility.

Right on ten minutes, Kirsten let the phone ring. The call was answered, not with the cheery, 'Hello,' but simply, a 'Yes?'

'Dom, been too long.'

'Not long enough,' said Dom. 'It came with a lot of heat. I hope you realised that.'

'A lot of heat?' asked Kirsten. 'For what? You guys were gone. You guys were out of the service.'

'And yet they still came in on the road one night. Got jumped, hood over the top, taken out, and interrogated.'

'For what?'

'Because they thought we were helping you. They thought you had called us and got us to help you with hiding whoever it was. We didn't appreciate it.'

'I wasn't bringing you into it,' said Kirsten. 'That's their call. That's their jumping to conclusions.'

'Well, you certainly pissed them off,' said Dom. 'Carrie-Anne struggles enough as it is. She's managed to get back to walking properly, managed to get herself up and ready again after that, well, the incident.'

The incident Dom referred to was a particular shootout, and most of the team had got injured in one way or another. After that Dom and Carrie-Anne had called it quits, left the service, and gone off together to start a new life. Dom wasn't happy his past was coming back at him.

'I need your help,' said Kirsten.

'No,' said Dom, 'I'm out. I don't want it next time. I don't want somebody taking me off to a dark place with a gun in my face and asking me questions about something I know nothing about. If I'm now seen with you, they'll go further than that. I might even end up in the sidewalk somewhere.'

'No, you won't. I need your help. I've got nobody else. I'm out of the service.'

'Well, I did get that feeling,' said Dom, angrily. 'I got that feeling when they kept kicking me. When they kept punching me.'

'I'm sorry,' said Kirsten. 'Well, they forced my hand, but I never brought you up. I never indicated you would be involved.'

'I guess they just checked, didn't they? I can't help you.'

'Just tell me if you heard anything.'

'About what?'

'Zante, on a beach there, there was an attack.'

'No,' said Dom. 'Just a second.' Kirsten heard him shout something over to Carrie-Anne before he returned to the call. 'Is it important?'

'I'm calling you,' said Kirsten. 'Of course, it's important.'

'What is it, a case? I mean, have you gone private or something?'

'No,' said Kirsten. 'I'm out. I'm out. I took Craig and I ran. They were meant to leave us alone, but somebody's grabbed Craig.'

'What?' said Dom. 'Craig's been grabbed?'

'Grabbed from the beach while I wasn't there. Somebody knifed a mayor and then Craig got kidnapped. I think he was trying to step in and help.'

'Is it locals?' asked Dom.

'I think so,' said Kirsten. 'Can't be sure. I need help.'

'Hang on,' said Dom.

Kirsten sat in the silence waiting for Dom to come back on the call. He'd be talking to Carrie-Anne checking any news reports, but his question told Kirsten she was in with a shout. Dom would be worried that it wasn't locals. If there was someone coming after Kirsten, given that they'd worked closely together, they might come after Dom and Carrie-Anne.

'Kirsten, we're in Austria at the moment. Going to take us a while to get there.'

'You don't have to come down. It's okay. I just want somebody on the outside. Somebody that can look through the internet and delve into any records I need. It's going to be hard from here.'

'Do you know it's local?'

'It's not confirmed,' said Kirsten. It was the truth. She only suspected. She didn't know for certain. She also didn't know who was ultimately behind all this. It was one thing to say it was locals because they were the people who physically grabbed Craig but was there anything else going on behind that? Were they put up to it? She could never be sure.

'Send a text to this number. Use the rapture two codes and send a grid reference with it. You'll need to keep people off your back. We'll come over.'

'Okay,' said Kirsten. 'I was also attacked in our flat. I think it was the locals again, looking to shut me up or at least take me along with Craig. I suspect they just wanted Brits.'

'Well, if they did, they picked the wrong ones. We will come. Carrie-Anne is looking at the flights at the moment. Are you okay?'

'No. No, Dom, I'm not. I'm sick to the core, my mind racing through all the scenarios and I'm trying hard to keep focus.'

Dom let silence reign on the phone for a while before he asked, 'And what's your next step?'

'I've got nobody out here, Dom. I can't look to the agency to put out feelers. I'm going to have to go to the only source I know. Plan is to break into the police station, see what they know.'

'How's your Greek?' asked Dom.

'Poor.'

'It's a good job I'm bringing Carrie-Anne over then. Fluent to the core.'

'Of course, she is. Always fluent in everything,' said Kirsten. 'I do miss you guys.'

'No, you don't,' said Dom. 'I don't miss being out, but I want to make sure that this isn't something else. You've got us to the end of this, then we're back out.'

'Thank you, Dom. Say thank you to Carrie-Anne.'

'Don't do anything stupid. You don't want to make too much of a ruckus. You don't want people to start looking at you too deeply.'

'Dom, I had to dispatch them. I think there's four dead in the flat. It's gone beyond that.'

'Oh hell,' said Dom. 'Shall I come prepped?'

'I would,' said Kirsten, knowing what Dom meant. *Should he bring an armoury with him?* Kirsten had some around the island. One of the particular hides had plenty of weaponry, but she wouldn't go there. Not until she required it. At the moment, she wanted to go to the police station and that would be infiltration. She certainly wasn't going to have an all-out shooting match.

'Stay safe,' said Dom. 'Might take us a day, but we'll be there. Remember to send me those coordinates.'

'Rapture two protocol. Will do. Thank you, Dom. I mean it.'

Kirsten closed down the call and tossed the phone into the bag. She pulled her legs up tight again, wrapping the fleece around them. She'd been lying there, lying there while he rubbed her back. Lying there in a state of happiness she hadn't had for so long. Where did that go? If she'd been there, there would've been two of them. They couldn't have taken both of them with them. She'd have stopped it. She'd have . . .

The tears began to flow. She was a professional. She knew what she had to do, but right now she needed to let out all the anxiety, the worry, and the regret that was racing through her. This was the time to cry.

# Chapter 04

Kirsten felt slightly buoyed at Dom and Carrie-Anne coming to assist. She was feeling extremely alone, and at least the face of friends would be good. Even if Dom was blaming her for what had happened to him since he'd left the service, it had been a good team, and they had worked well with Kirsten, and with Justin Chivers as well.

There was no way she could reach out to Justin; he was an awkward man to understand and close to Anna Hunt. She wasn't sure if he even would speak to her now she was outside the service. If she did, maybe he would let something slip. He was certainly good while you were batting for the same side, but if you were out in the field on your own, she didn't feel she could trust him the way she could Dom and Carrie-Anne.

Before night fell, Kirsten had dressed herself in a long, cool skirt with flip-flops and a light pink top. She wore a large sun hat and had put on a blonde wig, a pair of large shades finishing off the ensemble and she believed it was harder for people to recognise who she was. She didn't know if she should try an accent because, in fairness, she wasn't great at them. Probably best not to speak, to just keep out of everyone's way.

She picked up an evening paper and managed to interpret

enough of the Greek to realise that the mayor had been knifed, someone else was missing and she could see that the name or at least the aliases of Craig and her weren't mentioned in the paper. In fact, there was nothing about the flat at all. Maybe it had been too late for the evening edition. There was, however, an enhanced presence of police around, although they didn't seem to be doing much.

She wasn't daft enough to return to the scene of either the flat or the initial attack, thinking that people would still be looking for her to do that, to try and understand what was going on. Instead, she caught the bus up to another village and conducted most of her investigations from there. It was also where the police station for the area was located. As she watched, she could see various teams being brought in, swelling the ranks of the officers there.

Kirsten returned back to her cave hideout, changing into black leggings and a long-sleeved top. The heat in Zante was much stronger than she was used to, but the night still got dark. She took a balaclava along with a small black rucksack, as she sought to infiltrate the police station. Instead of catching the bus up, she ran the five miles, almost enjoying it before she arrived in the outskirts of the town. It was alive with tourists, and she skirted through the back streets until she saw the rear of the police station. There was a man in a chef's outfit smoking away at the back. The station was clearly big enough to have a canteen. She wondered the best play for getting inside.

Kirsten sat up a tree watching what was going on for the next hour. Most of the police officers, as they came and went, parked at the rear of the station, striding in through a door that was activated by a key card. However, the kitchen door was left open, and the chef kept popping out for another cigarette. Kirsten found it all very relaxed, considering there'd been a local attack. Who was to say that they wouldn't come for the police station?

She clambered down from the tree, crept along behind a wall and decided she would head for the kitchen door to get inside. The hour was now midnight. Although the police station was still busy, large parts of it seemed to have lights switched off.

Quickly, she strolled across the yard at the back, making for the kitchen door. As she approached it, she heard someone inside and laid herself flat up against the wall beside it. A man walked out; taking a cigarette out of his pocket, he placed it up to his lips as he stepped two, three, four, five steps away from the door and lit it. Maybe he thought there was somebody there, for after he lit the cigarette he turned round. By then, Kirsten was well inside.

The kitchen was well lit, so she strode across it, quickly opening a door at the far end that led into a corridor. She closed the door, ran along to an alcove, and then stood inside listening intently. She looked across at some signage and could make out the words Chief of Police, at least, she thought that's what it said. His office was further down the corridor. Maybe it was way further down the corridor, but she also saw the word stationery in their language and a sign which she thought meant front desk. She really needed to brush up on her Greek.

Kirsten pinned herself in tight to the alcove as she heard voices approaching along the hallway. There were two police officers describing some woman they'd picked up. Apparently, she was old and something else that Kirsten didn't catch. They walked past her. She hid in the alcove, and she saw the hand motions indicating that the woman was rather large. It was good though, for they were engaged with each other, not thinking about anyone being near them. She watched as they continued down the corridor before opening a door off to somewhere else.

Kirsten listened again. She couldn't hear anyone, so she strode quickly along. As she neared a corner, she took a mirror out on a long stem and quickly placed it around the corner to see who was there. The corridor was empty, so she ran round until she heard a noise at the far end.

She opened the nearest door and stepped inside a room with computers. The screens were on, but the lights weren't. She looked around for somewhere to hide. There was a gap underneath the tables, and she pushed herself into the far corner wrapping herself up tight. Then it occurred to Kirsten, what would she do if she got caught? She didn't want to pull a gun out; after all, this was the police. She was quite happy that she could conduct hand-to-hand combat and probably take most of them on but ideally, all contact would be avoided.

The door of the room opened, the lights came on, and she watched a young female officer sit down at the computer. The woman seemed to be growling and swearing. For the next five minutes, Kirsten watched her angrily type something into the computer. Afterwards, she stood up, walked to the end of the room, pulled a piece of paper from a printer before walking back out and closing the door, switching the lights off in the process. Kirsten held her position for another five minutes.

Satisfied that nobody else was coming in and the woman wasn't returning, Kirsten pulled herself out from underneath the table, approached the door and listened carefully. When she thought she could hear no one, she opened the door slightly, sending her mirror out and checking there was no one in the corridor. She ran quickly down the corridor and saw an office that she believed to be the Chief of Police's.

In front of it, there seemed to be a secretary's office which was now locked. Kirsten reached into her bag, pulled out a number of keys, and lockpick tools, and spent the next thirty seconds opening the door. She stepped inside and locked it from the inside. She then reached into the bag and took a small device that looked like a suction cup, placing it up against the wall.

A man was speaking fairly loudly to someone on a phone call. With the device Kirsten attached to the wall also connected to her phone, it allowed her to run an earpiece and to hear the conversation more clearly. The difficulty she had was he was chuntering along in Greek at a pace that she was uncomfortable with. There seemed to be lots of expletives as well, and the police chief also seemed to be angry.

'Why should I talk to you?' was one of the phrases that Kirsten caught. 'I'm the Police Chief,' another. 'Not here,' was another one. Kirsten continued to listen but saw on a desk beside her some copies of a recent report. There was a Post-it note on it indicating it was for the attention of the police chief. When she flipped the page over, she saw the names of their aliases Greg and Anne, who were apparently under investigation by the police. A case had been opened. She saw the word terrorist, saw the name of the local beach, and realised from the report that the police were onto it. Anne was also described as missing; Greg, kidnapped.

Kirsten carefully replaced the paper as the conversation next door was getting more and more heated.

'Now? You want to see me now?'

She was sure that's what he said. He then told the other

person to go away in a much more impolite fashion and then something akin to, 'All right, I'm coming.'

Kirsten took her device off, put it in the bag and got her lockpick tools out quickly. She opened up the office door and listened, hearing the police chief put on a coat and leave his room in a hurry. Five seconds after he'd walked past the door, she came out of the office, closed the door, quickly worked with the lockpicks, this time taking only twenty seconds to lock the door properly before haring up the corridor.

She didn't know where the chief would be going. Hopefully, he'd pop into a toilet or something on the way. She ran quickly up the corridor, stopping at each turn to hear if anyone was there, but there was no one. As she reached the kitchen, she saw the chef opening ovens on the far side and didn't halt but took off through the kitchen and straight out the back door. It was a risk but one she had to take.

As soon as she stepped outside, she jumped up and grabbed a low roof, hauling herself up on top. She kept down low, searching for the front door, waiting to see if the police chief would come out of it. When he didn't, she scanned the rear as well, standing up occasionally, risking being seen so she could identify him.

He stepped out into a private car and drove out of the rear of the police station, taking a right turn. Kirsten looked at the streets around her. She saw a motorcyclist pulling into the street adjacent to the police station. She ran to the end of the roof, jumped down onto a lower one, and then straight down into the street where the motorcyclist suddenly braked as this black figure appeared before him. It wasn't something she wanted to do, but Kirsten had to follow that police chief.

The motorbike was still running as she stepped forward,

grabbed the man, and pulled him as hard as she could. Kirsten didn't hesitate, reached down, grabbed the bike, jumped on, and sped off. As she turned right into the street in front of her, she saw the police chief's car making a left further up. She had him in her sights and breathed a sigh of relief.

Tailing the policeman wasn't that difficult. The chief took a road that led out towards the centre of the island before cutting off up a dusty track. Kirsten followed, keeping the sound of the car close to her, and turning off her own headlights as she raced along behind him. She saw the lights of his car stop some distance ahead so she drove off the track, left the bike underneath some trees, and ran as hard as she could up to where the lights were still on.

When she got there, she bent down a good one hundred metres out, scanning the area around her. From her bag, she took out infrared goggles, searched the area and saw there were at least six men out there. It'd be awkward getting close, but Kirsten believed she could do it and slowly made her way past a number of orange trees and got closer to the cars. From out of her bag, she pulled the listening device, and pointed it towards the conversation that was going on. The earpiece gave her a sketchy idea of the conversation.

Opposite the police chief was a tall man, impressive in stature, and he was definitely leading the conversation. The police chief, while not looking completely out of shape, certainly had a slight belly to him and was on the back foot. The other man seemed to be telling him that he knew nothing, that despite his investigations, the police chief knew nothing at all, and all enquiries were going to run into a dead end.

To the police chief's credit, he stood toe to toe with the man, asked him how he could possibly do that, but then a package arrived and was placed at the feet of the police chief. Kirsten watched him unzip it, take out a number of notes and started flicking through them. Kirsten had no idea how much money was in there, but the police chief mentioned something about there being a British man missing, something about it not being easy. The stranger put a hand up and then said something about it being important, then something about dead men and their identity going no further.

Kirsten watched the police chief nod his head. He picked up the money, walked back to the car and threw it onto the back seat. The other man then shouted over at him. Something akin to, 'We won't need to speak again, will we?' The police chief shook his head, stepped inside the car, and drove off back down the road he'd come up.

Kirsten held her ground and put on her infrared goggles to see where the other men were disappearing to. They walked away from the point of the meeting and in a direction completely different to the road. She followed them from a distance before watching them get into two cars and disappear again. Her bike was back under the tree in the other direction, but at least she had something now. Whoever this person was, she had a face and someone of that note, she'd be able to find.

Slowly Kirsten made her way back to the motorcycle and drove it back into the town she'd stolen it from. She left it on the outskirts, wiping it down as best she could to remove any fingerprints and then walked the five miles back to her cave. When she clambered inside that night, she wrapped herself up under some clothes trying to ignore the cold air of the cave. For a while, all thoughts of Craig had gone from her mind. She'd been back on mission, but now here, in the cold cave, all thoughts were about him. The previous night, he'd been wrapped around her; tonight, he was further from her than he'd been in the last two months and part of her wondered if she'd ever see him again.

# Chapter 05

Kirsten stepped out of the cave the next day, dressed like any old tourist with a shock of red hair. She wore large sunglasses, obscuring her eyes, and had decided to wear trainers rather than flip flops. It didn't quite fit the persona, but they were far easier to run in if she needed to get away. She also didn't carry a gun, which made her incredibly uneasy, but which also made it far easier to pass for a tourist. She could have hidden one deep inside her bags, but she wanted to be able to explain and talk things out. If she had a weapon on her, she'd more than likely end up using it.

Kirsten spent the first part of the day walking through the large town nearby, cruising along in front of clubs and other evening venues, restaurants, and eateries, often walking down the back alleys. She had picked up a small disposable camera, often pointing it up at what she pretended to be quite stunning architecture high up. However, in this part of the town, most of the buildings were fairly modern. The most unique part of the architecture was often where a third story hadn't been built, even though the interior structure had been built for it. There were bits of metal sticking out from the top of the roofs giving some houses the distinct impression they weren't finished.

Kirsten had always found that despite the fact that most criminal activity happened at night, there was a part of the day when criminals would meet, even if it was just on a social level—a time for plans or times to eat lunch together and talk about previous exploits. This often took place in various eateries or clubs when the doors were shut.

As she toured the streets, she watched for the right sort of people making their way inside of these buildings. In wandering the streets, she recognised one of the men from last night. It wasn't the leader, the main gangster; instead, it was one of his cohorts. Kirsten carefully tailed the man until she saw him disappearing into an eatery. Once he was inside, Kirsten stood across the street, looking at postcards with her eyes darting to and fro, watching who else was entering the building. Sure enough, his boss approached shortly afterwards.

They were sat in the middle of a restaurant, the large open window giving a good view of them. The boss was sitting with his back to her, so she couldn't lip-read what he was saying. From what she could make out from the other man who was sat with him, there wasn't anything of use. General banter. They certainly weren't talking shop.

Kirsten disappeared inside the shop where the postcards were, watching the men from a distance, picking up various items, but, all the time, glaring through different racks to see what was going on at the restaurant. When the leader had finished his lunch, Kirsten followed him across town, through various streets until he came to a nightclub. He disappeared inside, and Kirsten grabbed hold of one of the bouncers.

'Who is that?' she asked him. 'That looks like somebody I

know from school.'

'No, that's Manuel. He owns this club and various others. It's certainly not someone from school. Please, go on,' said the man.'

Kirsten got the feeling the man was trying to ward her off, which was good because Kirsten believed this was the nightclub that the leader would most likely frequent. She watched the club for the rest of the day, but the man didn't exit. She decided she would have to stay, but she also needed to get closer when the nightclub opened.

In the bag over her shoulder, she carried some evening wear, knowing that she may have to become more of a tourist on the street rather than your everyday mom clipping about on a holiday. Kirsten found some public toilets, made her change as darkness fell, and stepped out in a pair of long slacks and a strapless top. She had to look the part. Still, Kirsten was careful not to be the girl that everyone would be staring at. After all, she was sneaking in quietly.

Around about nine o'clock, believing that he hadn't left yet, Kirsten entered the building, smiling calmly at the bouncers on the door. She ignored their look back, striding in confidently, and heading up to the bar, ordering herself a large cocktail. Almost immediately as she did so, a man slid in beside her, introducing himself as Alan from Newcastle and asking her, 'Are you here on your own?'

'Why? Are you looking for a group of us, Alan? That's a bit frisky.'

Alan laughed. 'I can see you like your drink,' he said. 'Why don't you get that one down and I'll buy you another one.'

'That would be quick,' said Kirsten. 'My name's Lisa. I can tell you're from up north though.'

'You're from further north. I think I detect a Scottish accent in there.'

Kirsten hadn't tried to hide it, so, yes, he did. Sitting there, she listened to Alan talk on, telling her all about his exploits in the rugby team, what he did for a living, something to do with personal finance, and then how he was getting back on his feet after his divorce. He was giving quite possibly some of the worst chat-up lines she'd ever heard, but she didn't mind. He was good cover.

She positioned herself so she could look past his shoulder to the doors of the nightclub management beyond. At around about eleven o'clock and three cocktails later, Kirsten saw the gangster she'd seen the previous night step out into the club and look around, checking if everything was to his satisfaction. He stared across the main floor, and Kirsten clocked an older woman, possibly in her late fifties. She wasn't dressed like everyone else. Instead, she had a tight, long skirt on, and a blouse that seemed incredibly formal for where she was. Her hair was also tied up.

As she stood up, Kirsten could identify a gun hidden underneath the skirt. Kirsten laughed at one of Alan's jokes and almost swayed slightly, trying to get a better view of what the woman was doing as she approached the gangster. There seemed to be a brief embrace before the gangster pointed the woman to the door he'd come in through earlier.

'Should we dance, Alan?' asked Kirsten, and she grabbed his hand, taking him out in the middle of the floor. The music being played was quite modern, certainly none of her style, and she'd have been happier thrashing, head banging away, to some loud rock music. However, she went with whatever was on at this time. It was light, it was disco-y, and, frankly, she thought it was rubbish.

Alan jumped into the fray, dancing around like somebody who didn't know what music was, smiling incredibly at her. She wondered if it was about to go out of fashion. As he did so, she watched the gangster disappear through the back door, into whatever lay beyond, and she saw a large man step across the door. Kirsten knew she had to get inside quick, so she stepped forward, throwing her arms around Alan, planting a kiss on the side of his neck, biting him, reaching up and tugging at his ear.

'We can go now, if you want,' he said, displaying his keenness. Kirsten reached up closer, putting her hands around the back of his neck. Swiftly and out of sight, she hammered two fingers in, striking a nerve and causing Alan to suddenly collapse. Kirsten stepped back, hands to her face.

'What's wrong with him?' she screamed. 'What's wrong with him?' She turned and looked at the man guarding the door. 'Just don't stand there. Give him a hand.' The man looked panicked, not knowing what to do, but Kirsten ran to him, grabbing him by the arm. 'Come on, give him a hand. What is it?'

The man felt obliged to step forward. He reached down to see what was up with Alan, and Kirsten glided away from the fray where many of the punters were now standing, looking on. She slipped quickly to the door that was now left uncovered, shutting it behind her. She found herself in a corridor with a number of doors leading off it. As she walked quickly down it, up on her toes so as not to make any noise, she listened carefully, but it was hard to hear properly with the thumping dance beat going on outside. She leaned down by one door, heard nothing, then went to the next, then the one after that.

She could hear something and then heard a Russian's voice. It was a swear word and it was said with venom.

'I'm telling you the package is safe,' said the man. 'It's just the other half that's loose.'

'You were told to get both of them. We need both of them. We don't do these things for you for nothing, for free. We do them so you come in with your side of the deal.' Again, another swear word in Russian.

'Don't worry. We're looking for her. The police will find her if we don't. She's got nowhere to go.'

'You don't know who it is you're up against. We asked just you to bring them in.'

Kirsten ears pricked up at being told that they were being brought in. Were they meant to come for Kirsten as well? There was the attack at the flat. Was the idea with the mayor that Kirsten and Craig were going to be onlookers and grabbed as part of that? Was it part of the deal? Why were the Russians involved? Was this harping back to something she'd been involved in earlier? Was this harping back to Control and maybe her sister, the Huntress. She knew Control was dead, for Craig had killed her. As for the Huntress, the last Kirsten knew she was being dragged away in a near death state. She was being held, if not deceased, as far as Kirsten knew, by Godfrey, probably never to be let go. She was too dangerous for that. She'd come after them. Although, maybe he'd trade her back. As long as her paymasters knew what was going on, then she wouldn't react the way she had previously.

Kirsten continued to kneel down behind the door, listening intently until she could hear the door opening. Back in the nightclub, the music thumped again, much stronger. She looked around. Anyone coming down the corridor would see her within the next couple of seconds. She couldn't see her way out, just other offices. She could try the doors, but they might not even be open. In Kirsten's mind, she knew she had to leave the building as soon as possible.

However, she'd heard a Russian voice coming from the room and she wanted to know who it was. After all, 'It was a Russian voice', wasn't going to cut much weight. If she could get an image of the person, a picture, that might help. She could get Dom and Carrie-Anne to run some sort of recognition.

Kirsten stood up, took her phone from her pocket, put it onto the camera setting and then opened the door in front of her. She did it quickly, watched as the gangster and the Russian woman both turned around in shock and she fired a picture off of both.

Straight away, she shut the door, and pocketing the phone, she ran back up the corridor to meet two men coming towards her. Kirsten saw one reach for a gun and went straight for him, grabbing his head, smacking it off a wall. The other one went to grab her, but she'd reached down and grabbed the gun out of the first man's holster and caught the second man with the butt of it. She turned, pointed down the corridor where the gangster had just come around the corner. He saw her gun, spun back, throwing himself to one side as she shot. As soon as she fired the gun, the whole place went into uproar.

From behind her, on the dance floor, she could hear screaming, people running for cover. Kirsten fired two more up into the air. She grabbed hold of one of the men who'd come to attack her, picking him up and pushing him out in front of her as she went through the door onto the dance floor. A number of shots hit the man's body but she let him drop, firing back at those who'd fired at her. At least one had fallen, others had gone for cover.

Kirsten ran hard, sliding across a couple of tables towards one of the windows on the far side of the club. She fired the handgun she'd acquired, and the window smashed. She remembered that the club was on street level. As she reached it, she simply jumped up, put her shoulder into the remaining glass, and flew out of the window.

She was tight in a ball and then began to extend her feet where she thought the ground would be. They were a little bit late arriving because she hadn't realised that the road on this side of the club descended down a hill. It caught her unawares. When her feet landed, she tumbled forward rolling into a wall.

She stopped, lifted her gun up, and pointed it back at the window, firing twice again, before running off into the night. She could hear sirens in the town and took the red wig off, tucking it down her trousers. There was a small orange grove in front of a house, so she jumped the wall and hid in there. With there being a security gate on it, she thought it would be a good cover, and the police were less likely to check somewhere with a lock on it first, rather coming back to it later.

She heard the sirens in the night, and she waited, hidden amongst the trees, as the sounds of the night pervaded the air. She reckoned it was four in the morning before she jumped back over the wall and started walking out of town. It was six before she reached the cave, flopping down, desperate for a night's sleep but wondering who the Russian woman was.

*The package was safe though,* she thought. *Craig was safe. That was a relief. Why were the Russians involved though?* She pulled out her phone and looked at it. She didn't recognise the woman at all. Throughout her escapades with the service, no one like that had even come up in the photo books or during a mission. Kirsten put her head down, wondering what her next step should be. She'd need to talk to Dom. She needed to get back and to follow her gangster and see if he led her to Craig.

She realised, as she lay in the dark, that the hardest part of what she was doing was keeping that lingering doubt about Craig away from her mind. *He was alive. The man said he was safe.* Kirsten took out the other gun that she had acquired from the man at the club. She placed it in the bag to one side in the cave and then lay down, wrapping her arms around herself. This was when it was hardest, when she realised he wasn't there, every time she went to sleep.

# Chapter 06

Kirsten woke up in the cold cave and immediately tried to pull some more of her excess clothing over her. She wasn't sure if it was the chill inside or the thought that she might not see Craig again that was making her so cold. Or was it simply just being hidden from the sun? Either way, it had been a fitful night's sleep, and she tried to stretch a little. The extra clothing didn't appear to be warming her up any. The confines of the cave were tight, but Kirsten managed to stretch here and there before fumbling around in the dark and finding some of her food reserves. Having eaten and drunk some water, she crawled her way to the front of the cave, peering out at the beach ahead of her. No one was there. When she checked the time, it was ten in the morning. The sun was pointing at the cave and Kirsten let her face bathe in it briefly before pulling herself back inside.

Kirsten dressed in the garb of a tourist and allowed herself to walk along the beach to the far end, where she was out of sight of the main road. There was no one else around, indeed, no boats, even out on the sea so she took her mobile and sent a message to Dom. A call came back quickly.

'We're still on our way,' he said. 'I'm trying to do what work

I can before we get there.'

'Well, I've got some more work for you,' said Kirsten. 'I'm sending you a photograph of a woman. She met with the gangster who met with the police chief. She's Russian. I'm thinking it takes us back to the issue with the Huntress.'

'Well, that's a possible lead,' said Dom, 'but Russians could be there for many other reasons.'

'With the history we've got, I think it's a line that needs checked out. Either way, you need to find out who this agent is.'

'If indeed she is an agent,' said Dom. 'She might just be a Russian gangster herself, but you need to be careful.'

'Well, I know that,' said Kirsten.

'No, really be careful. The news has it out now that the local mayor was murdered by terrorists. They're now looking for an Anne. Apparently, Greg is missing. I take it that's you two.'

'Yes,' said Kirsten. 'But they're looking for me for what? They think I may have been taken as well?'

'No, they're looking at you as a potential murderer. You may have been involved in him being taken. They're basing that on the fact that a number of terrorists attacked your flat. You left quite a mess behind you.'

'Well, they didn't give me much choice,' said Kirsten. 'Are they saying that Craig's still alive?'

'Only that he's been kidnapped. They've not found a body. There's been no ransom demand, either.'

'If they're trying to frame me, do you think they're trying to flush me out?' asked Kirsten.

'Of course, they're trying to flush you out,' said Dom. 'If the Russians are involved and this has led back to the legacy of Control, then you need to be especially careful. But what I don't understand is if that's the case why not simply . . . '

'Simply what?' asked Kirsten.

'Simply kill off Craig, put a bullet in him. Why this thing with the mayor? What's all that about?'

'The mayor's been involved because of the terrorist group. I reckon that's their side of the bargain; think about it. It's been staged, hasn't it? It must be some way of coming in and getting at us.'

'I'm not convinced it's definitely that,' said Dom, 'There's too much uncertainty. We need to tread carefully. When Carrie-Anne and I get there, we can give you more feet on the ground.'

'That'll be nice; also, you can get me somewhere better to sleep. I'm sick of being on cold floors. It's not warm without . . . '

'Not warm without him,' said Dom. 'But you have to take away that sentimentality,' he said. 'You need to focus like you always do. Treat it like a job; otherwise, you'll not be as efficient.'

'I don't want to be efficient. I want to rip the place apart. That's how I'll find them, shake people down.'

'No,' said Dom, 'because if you're right about Control, that's how they find you. Maybe they want you because they want to harm you before they put you down, and Craig as well. Or maybe it is just terrorists, and the police chief does know what's going on and they're trying to make it look better because the tourists did it. I'm trying to see what other activity there is going on. My connections into Godfrey and the service are not . . . not what they used to be. Have you thought about contacting Justin Chivers?'

'I'm not going near Justin. Justin is too close to Anna. He owes her too much; besides, they could watch him. They were watching him much closer than they ever watched you. He's still in the service; he's still there.'

'I think you need to talk to someone. You may need more than us. I will, however, look into Control and what happened to her sister, the Huntress. Someone said she'd gone off to the prison. Still being held somewhere; maybe this is what it's about—get Craig and you hostage and ask to pass her back.'

'But we're not in the service anymore. Surely, they're going to know the service will just dump us. Especially after the last one; I went against them. That'll be known as that sort of thing doesn't stay quiet, Dom.'

'No, it doesn't and that's what's bothering me as well. You may be right; you may not get the backup that you deserve from the service.'

'How long until you get here?'

'Another day or two; just sorting out fake passports and preparing ourselves with some armoury. We don't move about as easily as we used to. We don't keep up the same number of hides and dens and identities. We were out longer than you were.'

'I know,' said Kirsten. 'I'm sorry to bring you back into it; there was nowhere else to go, Dom.'

'Don't worry,' he said. 'We'll be there with you; until then, keep your head down.'

'I always do.'

'Not according to the news. Bit of a fracas in a nightclub last night; guessing that was you.'

Kirsten laughed. 'Yes, that's where I met the Russian woman. See if you can find out who she is; could be the key to working at what's going on.'

'Maybe. Oh, Carrie-Anne sends her love.'

'Is she okay to come?' asked Kirsten knowing how the woman had been injured in the last mission together.

'I could give an opinion, but it would make no difference, she's coming. I was the one questioning the wisdom of it. She's coming.'

The call closed and Kirsten put the phone back into her pocket and looked out at the sea. It was blue turning to green as it got closer in, and you could see into the water. She thought about the water back in Scotland which, whatever time of the year you went into it, was cold. In some parts, it was indeed beautiful, and you could see the sea creatures below. Other parts weren't so nice, but here you could step in it; it would be warm, well, at least warm enough to walk around and paddle in. She stepped a couple of feet forward, and let the water run across her feet. She could feel the warmth of the sand even at this early hour.

What would Godfrey do with Control's sister? What would he have done with her? Had she survived? Was she taken off, taken away to be debriefed, interrogated? They wouldn't get that much from her. Then what—would he just dispatch her?

The woman was dangerous, so he wouldn't make a trade. Surely, they'd want her back, unless, of course, she'd run off unsanctioned, and then again, they might want her back to discipline her. Either way, Kirsten could see a spiral of anger coming out of it. Craig had shot Control dead, saving Godfrey's life in the process, but when her sister, the Huntress, had come for vengeance, Anna Hunt had been the one to take her down after the woman had almost ended Kirsten's team.

Kirsten flicked a little water up and hitched up the sarong she was wearing, stepping out into the water until it was up past her knees. She closed her eyes listening intently, but there was nothing around her except that gentle lapping of the water. There was a saying that being by the sea always calmed you with the way you saw things. She breathed in deeply.

*Macleod wouldn't be looking at all the action,* she thought; *he'd be looking at the reasoning, why take Craig?*

If there were people, supporters of the Huntress, would they be trying to get her back? If so, why would they take Craig and Kirsten? They weren't valuable anymore, they weren't current operations, and really, how much did she know now? If they took down Anna Hunt or Godfrey, you might be thinking it was the Russian services, but what had happened to Control's sister? If you want her exchanged, take Anna Hunt or Godfrey, take somebody high up, not Craig and not Kirsten, and not now they'd left. Why would you kidnap them both?

A horrible thought went through Kirsten's head; what if it were vengeance? What if somebody wanted to get Craig back for killing Control? What if they wanted Kirsten to harm her in front of Craig, make him suffer? That was a thing, wasn't it? Just remember those mafia films. If they actually liked you and you were a good egg, they came up behind you and killed you without you even knowing. But if you'd wronged them badly as they saw it, you'd suffer before you died. Dom and Carrie-Anne would come up with the answers. They would. They'd have to. She knew what was really driving that comment into her head.

Justin Chivers had been like her right-hand man. He was terrific at all this sort of thing: finding out what was happening in the Service community, who was doing what, diving into records he had no right to be in, helping establish the fuller picture. Deep down, she knew she didn't trust Justin that much. Now she'd left, and he was still in the Service, she reckoned he'd run down to Anna Hunt with this. Run and tell her. If he did, what would the Service think?

For a start, Craig and Kirsten were out of the Service. There was also the fact that the Service might not want them to speak about previous missions. Could they dispatch a kill order on them? They weren't shy about kill orders. Suddenly she wondered if the terrorists that had infiltrated the flat had actually been terrorists. Could they have been from the Russians? Could they have been from the locals? Could they have been from the British Service?

Kirsten continued to walk through the water, pushing it apart with her knees. It rose up wetting the bottom of her sarong. She reached down into the pocket of the shorts she had on underneath, taking the phone out, holding it in her hands, making sure it wouldn't get wet. She walked quickly through the water, pushing hard, allowing it to rise up across her thighs, eventually splashing up onto her belly and hips. When she had walked a good one hundred metres in one direction, she turned and went back, this time quicker, eventually trying to break into almost a run, having to drive her legs through the water. She then stopped, walked out of the water, and lay down on the sand. She didn't know why she did that. Maybe she just needed a break for a moment; maybe she needed to do something mindless, to tune out.

Something in the back of her mind said this was from before. This was a legacy of actions she'd taken in the Service. The action was now costing Craig. It might even cost him his life. Kirsten sat up on her elbows and looked out to the water, her back to anyone that would come along the beach, to whatever road ran up to the top where they could vaguely see her. She made sure her back stayed there, not because she didn't want to be identified, but because she didn't want anyone to see the tears that were now streaking down her face.

She'd get him back. She'd get him back if it was the last thing she did. She'd make them pay. She'd damn well make them pay.

# Chapter 07

After having a weaker moment, as she liked to think of it, looking out to sea and crying, Kirsten returned to the cave and got dressed into a pair of slacks and a t-shirt before taking a small rucksack and walking into town. She returned to the nightclub, watching it from across the road in a small cafe. She had a blonde wig on and a much older look about her. Today she was a backpacking tourist, and this allowed her to watch undetected.

The doors were closed and she saw several men come and go, as well as the occasional cleaner or worker. The first two hours she was there, she didn't see the gangster, but then he arrived, disappearing inside. Kirsten decided to remain watching from the small cafe. She wondered if she could break in, put a gun to the guy's head, but then again, she didn't know where Craig was. That was the big problem. Anything she did, especially if they saw it as being her, could put Craig in danger. As long as they had him somewhere she didn't know, they could always threaten her. Kristen wondered what the best thing was to do and then felt her mobile phone vibrating. She saw a text message and called the number to find Dom on the other end.

'We'll be there soon' said Dom, 'but I did make some contacts regarding the Huntress. It wasn't easy, but a few people have the jitters about them, especially seeing what's going on around you.'

'What do you mean?' asked Kirsten.

'Anybody involved in that situation is too reserved about it as it appears she didn't make it anywhere else. She didn't go back to Russia. There're rumours there was a trade, that they were going to exchange her for someone else. The person they were exchanging her for has turned up. I've been able to clarify that, that he was brought back in exchange for someone else, but my source says the paperwork's dodgy because they say he was exchanged for a Russian woman, except the Russian woman they're talking about on the paper went on a completely different exchange. You see, my source was there for that exchange.'

'So, what? She just never left the country? You're saying the Huntress is still there?'

'Nope. She's not been held anywhere. There's no record of her. She is gone.'

'What do you mean, she's gone?'

'Exactly what I'm saying. She's gone. It would be my bet that Godfrey deemed her too dangerous, but you'll only get the real story by going to him, which isn't going to happen, or by getting hold of Anna Hunt. As much as she was angry at you leaving, you and Anna Hunt have a bond. She gets you, Kirsten. She believed in you. She put you up in front of Godfrey. She was the one that recommended you. Anna has a lot of good thoughts about you, so I think it's worth making contact.'

'No! No way,' said Kirsten; 'contact Anna, she won't be happy you and Carrie-Anne are involved. Besides I don't want her knowing you are. If this goes wrong, if somehow the service is on the opposite side of this, I don't want you being hunted. You left on an amical basis, both of you. I didn't. There's no need for you to be under the cloud I am.'

'Look, this is about Craig and we're both agreed. We're happy to go get him. If that means we have to go in and risk a few things, that's what we do.'

'No,' said Kirsten. 'I want to keep you safer than that. You're coming over, great, but let's make sure they don't know you're here . . . anyone.'

'Then you're not going to get to the bottom of this. You need to go and ask someone. We need to find out who did this. Did someone dispatch the Huntress? Because if they did, then there could be a world of grief coming your way.'

'And your way, too, if you're coming to help me. No, don't go and ask Anna. Let's ask via the side door. I'll call Justin. I'll make the contact. I'll keep you out of it at the moment. That way, if anything happens to me, you're still available to go get Craig.'

'Okay,' said Dom, 'I can run with that and we'll be there soon.'

Kirsten continued to watch the club, but the gangster didn't come out. Kirsten wondered what she should do. She could go in there, put a gun to the man's head and try and find out where Craig was. But if she did that, and he wasn't the one holding him, she could very easily have lost her best line of getting to him. At some point, the gangster might pay a visit to Craig, or at least take Kirsten to someone who knew where he was. He, himself, could know where Craig was.

It was frustrating her playing a watching game, but it was a smart move at the moment. Roughing anyone up just drew attention to herself. Kirsten pulled out her phone and dialled a number. The other end rang six times and Kirsten closed the call. She rang again, allowing it to ring six times and closed the call. The third time she rang, it was answered after three rings.

'Why are you calling me?' said the voice on the other end.

'Because I need help.'

'It doesn't work like that anymore, Kirsten, does it? You're on the outside now. I can't just run around helping you. You know that they keep tabs on me, what I'm doing.'

'Yes, I do, but you're good. You're very good and they don't watch you that closely, at least not close enough. You've always been able to get info.'

'But you were my boss then,' said Justin. 'I was doing it for the greater purpose. What do I need to do for you now?'

'Craig's been kidnapped.'

'Zante. That's you in Zante, isn't it?'

'Craig's been kidnapped,' Kristen reiterated. 'I need assistance. It seems that there's Russian involvement. I need to know if it's the Huntress, or someone linked to her. The only history I've got of Craig and I being involved with the Russians is on this side. That's where the grudge will come from for him to be kidnapped. They say a terrorist took him, but it's not washing with me. We haven't had a ransom demand yet. They haven't paraded him. They killed the mayor right in front of him. I think I was meant to be taken as well, but I reckon they stuffed up. Somebody came after me. They aren't coming after me anymore, but I've got an entire police force looking for me. I've got a gangster who's involved with the Russians, and I know they have Craig somewhere, and I need some help to know what that Russian involvement might be. I need you to go to Anna Hunt and find out if Godfrey took out the Huntress.'

'Wow,' said Justin, 'just hold on a moment. You're asking me to find out if Godfrey went dark on some of this by asking Anna? She's still pissed at you. Godfrey is pissed at Anna because she recommended you. I've been keeping well away from all those subjects.'

'And doing what?' asked Kirsten.

'Just a lot of desk work, and feeding into situations. I've been keeping away from Anna and Godfrey as much as possible. What you did came back on the rest of us. You do realise that in this game if you spend time with someone and they turn, you don't get looked at the same.'

'This is Craig's life I'm talking about,' said Kirsten. 'I don't care what reputations do or don't get sullied. I need to save him. After all he'd done for the Service, you think they'd be out here.'

'What's to say they aren't? What's to say they're not involved?' asked Justin. 'Think out of the box. Think bigger.'

'Just talk to Anna for me, all right? See what she knows.'

'I haven't been able to reach her recently, but okay. I can get hold of her, but she's going to be pissed, and you're going to have to accept that she might come after you. She might come in and intervene, especially if they think it's Craig and you.'

'If you've worked out it's Craig and me,' said Kirsten, 'what's to believe that they haven't? Why wouldn't they be here already if that was the case?'

'Look,' said Justin, 'I'll have a look. I'll see what I can do. I'll try and talk to Anna on the quiet, but like I said, I don't work directly for her at the moment, and I haven't been able to be in touch. I've got no reason to be in touch with her and that's why I haven't gone near her. Part of her half blames me since

I was working with you.'

'Thanks, Justin.'

'You haven't involved anyone else, have you?'

'No,' said Kirsten, very deliberately.

'That's understood. A very wise move. I'll be in touch.'

Kirsten closed the call and looked over to the nightclub. She watched a blonde woman approach. She seemed to struggle to speak the language of the man who was on guard duty protecting the outside of the building. There was a little confusion, the one where people who speak another language try to talk to a native and don't quite follow. She could see it on their lips, the faces, the way they looked at each other, almost with incomprehension. Then she was led inside.

Kirsten stood up from her table, crossed the road calmly, and walked to the side of the nightclub. Then she walked around the rear of it. She saw a couple of men lingering by the gate who were clearly there to stop anyone from going in, and Kirsten walked straight past them ignoring the cat calls they gave as she strolled along. She walked along the back of all the other buildings until she could cut up through an alley and back onto the main street. She wandered back to the front of the nightclub and wondered how she would get in. Looking across the street, three shops down was a closed door. Kirsten looked up at the roofs. There was a bit of a height difference. She could get down, but it was daylight. It would be difficult to do it discreetly, but that was an option.

Kirsten strolled over the street into a clothes shop and began browsing around. She filtered slowly towards the back of the store and then disappeared out through a door that led upstairs. The stairway was extremely plain, white walls, obviously for coolness with the temperatures outside. There was no mark on the walls from boxes or people scraping past.

The flooring was wooden, and she carefully walked up, trying her best not to make any sound. There were several doors on the first floor, and she crouched down while she walked past them before taking the flight up to the second. The same arrangement was on the second floor, more doors with a glass pane in them, and Kirsten had to walk low to nip underneath those windows.

When she went up the third steps, however, she was able to open a door onto the roof. Again, she kept low walking across to the roof edge where she saw a small drop down onto the next roof. Kirsten took it easily, landing on top of the dusty rooftop and crept her way past the air conditioning units that sat on top. When she got to the edge of it, she saw there was a small gap between the roof of the nightclub and this building. She would also drop about six or seven feet.

She looked around for anything to bridge the gap over. There wasn't anything. She took several steps backwards, looked at the ledge of the roof in front of her, and sprinted hard at it. She planted her left foot on top of it, pushed hard, flinging both arms forward. Kirsten landed on the rooftop of the nightclub rolling forward, her backpack going underneath her and making it incredibly uncomfortable before she was able to roll back to her feet. She stopped briefly, looked around to see if anyone had noticed, but there was no one there.

Kirsten crept over to a door in the middle of the roof. It was locked and she took out some lock picks from her rucksack, opening the door in thirty seconds and then closing it behind her. The stairs she descended were concrete and she walked slowly down them wondering what she would find. Once the door closed behind her, it was dark. Although she saw a light switch, she didn't want to switch it on and alert anyone below. She descended the first flight of stairs and found herself in a landing with several offices. She opened the first door, entered a dark room and found a number of cardboard boxes. She pulled back the lid on an open one, put her hand inside, and pulled out a white powder and plastic bags.

Part of her wanted to burn it up. Clearly, the drugs were for the local area, but Craig was the point of this visit, nothing else. Kirsten exited the room and continued down the concrete steps until she came to another landing. She slid along the wall, listening carefully for anyone and then peeked quickly with her mirror through the window of the first door. She saw the gangster with the blonde woman who had entered the nightclub earlier.

She heard him say something about taking her somewhere after lunch and Kirsten wondered exactly where they were going. She heard the word prisoner in Greek and then another word, something she thought meant captive though she wasn't too sure. The pair stood up suddenly and Kirsten ran back to the concrete stairs, running up the flight until she was out of sight, and then placing her mirror so she could clock the pair coming out of the door.

The blonde woman was young, the gangster somewhat older, and she watched a stray hand of his being placed on the woman's backside as she left. His hand then rose and was on her shoulder, and she wondered if he was sweet talking her or if she was allowing herself to be spoken to like this, drawing his confidence in. They had said they were going for lunch, then they were going somewhere.

Kirsten took the mirror away, placing it back inside her backpack and climbed the steps to the roof. She followed the edge round and looked down at the rear of the club and saw the gangster's car he'd been in several nights previous. She sat down on her backside just out of sight of the door that led to the concrete steps. From her current position she could see if he left and so she would wait for him to finish his lunch and take the blonde woman to wherever this captive or prisoner was.

# Chapter 08

Justin Chivers stood in front of the mirror in a large department store, adjusting the tie around his neck. It was yellow, but a more intense yellow, and although it was a colour he normally would go for, it wasn't growing on him. Slowly, he undid the knot, hung the tie back up and chose another one. This one was a light blue, and once again after he'd tied it on, he felt it really wasn't him.

He placed both ties back on the appropriate racks and undid the top button of his shirt before strolling around the department store. He had decided to take an hour off, because frankly, he was a little bit disturbed by what Kirsten had said that morning. He tried afterwards to contact Anna Hunt but with no success and he had been using the more private lines of communication Anna kept, the ones for very urgent comments.

As he walked along, he saw a lady with a large white handbag. She must have been over seventy, with tightly permed white hair, but when he looked over at her, she very quickly looked the other way. Justin gave a wry smile, turned to look to the other side of him and he saw a young man in his twenties who apparently was very keen on a shirt you would normally see on an old man.

Justin continued to walk. He took himself into the women's section of the department store, heading directly for the underwear. He stopped, picking up a rather large bra, holding it up to the light, turning it round as if he was studying it intensely. It was the last thing Justin was doing. His own sexuality would never demand looking out for a bra like this even for a lover, but more than that he was trying to see if anyone else would be joining him in this section. The woman had disturbed him. The man looking at the wrong type of shirt for his age.

Justin looked beyond the bra he was holding up and clocked the man suddenly becoming very interested in women's underwear. He was holding three different sets, and Justin could tell that one of them was distinctly a different size to the others. He put the bra back on the rack, walked on, and then turned around suddenly looking behind him.

There were four men in the section, all suddenly studying ladies' underwear with incredible intent. You might see one, maybe two. One would usually be asking an assistant for sizes. No man would sit like this looking intently without being embarrassed or awkward. Certainly, out of the four, at least half of them would be.

Justin continued to walk through the ladies' section, and every now and again, would stop. The old white-haired woman was there again, and he saw a man who had previously been looking at women's underwear. He strolled quickly out of the department store onto London Street. He cut back along the side of one of the parks. Once he'd turned the corner and was out of sight, he began to run, umbrella still at his side. From in front of him at the entrance to the park, two men appeared, both of them, six feet tall and with muscles that Justin could only wish for.

He turned around on his heel and wanted to run back, but three men were coming from that direction. He turned to the pair in front of him. As he got close, one reached for him, but Justin held up his umbrella in front of him, pressing a button and firing a small dart into the man. He collapsed quickly, but the other man was on Justin, now grabbing the umbrella. Justin drove his heel onto the man's toes, saw him grimace a little, but then the man reached for Justin.

Justin was still holding on to the umbrella with one hand. He then pressed the second button down from the one that had activated the dart. Quickly, Justin let go of the umbrella as it suddenly became charged, and the man holding it received a shock of significant proportion, so much so that it made him tumble to the ground.

Justin wanted to run, but those behind him had caught up, and one grabbed his shoulder. Justin threw an elbow in the man's face, while the second put his arms around Justin, pulling him back by the waist. Justin wanted to swing another elbow round, but this time, a gun was placed on Justin's head.

'Seems the boss wants a word with you. Kindly step in,' said a cockney voice. A black limousine pulled up on the nearby road, and the rear door was pushed open. Justin was bundled hard inside, and a black hood placed over his head. His hands were taken and a plastic tie forced them together.

'Just sit there and shut up,' said the cockney voice again. Justin heard the door close, and the car drove off.

'Do you mind if I sit up if it's going to be a long journey without pleasantries?  Oh, and don't forget to bring my umbrella as well.'

Scene Break Scene break Scene Break

Justin recalled the steps he'd been taken along. He'd gone down two sets of stairs and turned left, walked along. He reckoned at least three hundred steps before a door had opened in front of him and he'd been thrown into what he believed was some sort of cell. It was damp and cool enough. He was placed on a plastic chair, and he reckoned there was a table in front of him because he had lifted his knees and touched something wooden. He still had the hood on, damp and affecting his breathing. He'd sweated quite a bit underneath the hood and along with the stillness of the air in the cell, he felt he wasn't ready to take a deep lungful of the stale air around him.

He heard the door of his presumed cell open. It closed with a clunk. Someone sat down on the chair opposite, he believed, for he heard it scratch backwards, and some papers or something was placed on the table.

'Mr Chivers, I felt I needed a word with you.'

*Oh hell*, thought Justin, *Godfrey*. Godfrey was the head of the service, and if Godfrey wanted a word with you, you were in trouble. Normally, if you were working for him, he was very approachable, albeit he demanded a level of professionalism that many didn't attain. Justin had never been someone that Godfrey had got on the wrong side of. Justin was a professional. Even when he broke into places and computers that he shouldn't have, he did, at least, know where that information shouldn't go to.

'Earlier on today, you received a call from Kirsten Stewart. Tell me about the conversation.'

Justin could feel himself sweating, but he controlled his breathing trying not to show any fear or worry.

'Do you think we could dispense with the hood? I know who it is. I know where I am. I'm not going to make a run for it.'

'You couldn't make a run for it if you tried in here, so it's not an unreasonable request and I can look you in the eye.'

Justin heard Godfrey stand up, walk around and the hood was quickly removed. Disturbingly, Godfrey took his time to fold the hood and place it on the table. Justin then tried to indicate the hands that were tied behind his back, for comfort's sake, as he put it, but Godfrey sat down again in his own seat, opposite.

'I want to look you in the eye, I didn't say I wanted to give you the opportunity to come at me. Many people underestimate you, Mr Chivers. I do not. I do not underestimate many people. You'll stay with your hands tied until I know what I want to know and then I'll decide if you're going back out into the world or not.'

'You're asking if I received a phone call today from Kirsten Stewart. Yes, I did.'

'And what was Miss Stewart saying to you? Something about holidays?'

'Kirsten was ringing me because she's worried. A former operative and her current boyfriend is missing. It appears that they were out in Zante.'

'I know they've been out in Zante. They've been followed ever since she left us. What else do you know about them?'

'I know that there's been an attack on a mayor out there and the mayor died. Your former operative tried to get involved and was kidnapped. He's not being held up for ransom. There's not been anything asked about him. Poor Kirsten is trying to find him. She was attacked as well at their flat.'

'Thank you, Mr Chivers, for updating me on what I already knew. What is she doing?'

'She's trying to work out what's going on. She's trying to work out if it's you that's caused this problem.'

'Me, Mr Chivers? Why on earth would she think that it's me that's causing a problem?'

'Kirsten's investigating,' said Justin, 'but she believes there may be some Russian involvement.'

There was a flicker on Godfrey's face. Most people would've missed it and he tried to cover it up as quickly as he could, but there was that flicker, and Justin grinned.

'She believes that the Russians are involved. She's just not sure which Russians and she was asking me to find out about the Huntress. Was she still here in a lockup somewhere or had she been traded?'

'What did you do about that?'

'I tried to contact Anna Hunt, but she's not responding. I do, of course, know the rumours.'

'What rumours?' asked Godfrey. 'We can't have rumours running around. Rumours get people killed.'

'The rumour is that you did the killing.'

'I'm always rumoured to have killed people, but I don't take credit for things I haven't done.'

'But you'll take credit for this one.' Justin watched the man look away. 'Let's not kid ourselves, Godfrey. I'm here because you need something. What's the matter?' Godfrey stared at the face opposite him, but Justin remained completely impassive. 'It's Anna, isn't it?'

There was that flicker again, and then Godfrey stood up, walking about the cell.

'Where's Anna? What's up with her?'

'Oh, that's quite some emotion,' said Godfrey.

'I owe Anna. I may have disagreed with her on things, but I owe her. Where is she?'

'You owe her things. You mean like the fact she's allowed you to keep up a persona of being a heterosexual male, and in fact, you're homosexual. The whole palaver of Justin the office slime ball chasing around the women.'

'Where is Anna?' asked Justin and noticed Godfrey's arm was shaking slightly.

'Anna is missing,' said Godfrey. 'She was out in that region on the Greek mainland but travelling. She was following up on something that had been given to us.'

'It must have been a deal to send Anna,' said Justin.

'Seemed almost too good to be true. It looks like it was. I was bothered when Anna hadn't reported in,' said Godfrey, 'but these things happen in our profession, so I wasn't too worried until I saw the reports from Zante.'

'Where is the Huntress?' asked Justin.

'The woman was too dangerous,' said Godfrey. 'You tell anybody else that, and you'll find out how dangerous I am.'

'So, this could be vengeance? This could be . . .'

'We don't know what this is, but I know that Anna Hunt is missing, and I do not know what's in Anna Hunt's head to go to anyone else.'

'But if Craig's missing and Anna's missing, maybe . . .'

'Yes, maybe. I think you're going to go and get on a flight, Mr Chivers. I think you're going out to Zante. I want you to assist as best as you can, and I want Anna Hunt back.'

'What about Craig and Kirsten?' asked Justin.

'If that pair look like they're about to be taken off to the custody of another state, kill them. However, if they seem to be fending for themselves, and will once again be free to knock about this world, then so be it. That's your orders. Get me Miss Hunt and get those two to a safe place, or get them six feet under. You have the disposal of the department. I'll get someone in here to let you out soon.' Godfrey turned away towards the door, but as he opened it, Justin spoke.

'I won't kill them. You understand that.'

'Well, it seems like Kirsten got to all of you.'

'But why would you send me out?' asked Justin. 'You could just send a hitman and kill everyone. Make sure nothing gets away.'

'Frankly, Anna Hunt is too valuable to let slip away in any form, and as for Kirsten, she's liable to avoid a hitman but she may just get to the bottom of all this. That's why you're going out to supervise and to watch. Assess, do what's necessary but understand I want Anna Hunt back. The other lot, I don't care as long as they're not leaking anything.'

Justin gave a nod and then watched Godfrey close the door behind him. Inside, his mind was racing. *Anna Hunt was missing. Somebody had set up Anna Hunt, Craig, and they were looking for Kirsten. Did that mean at some time they can come for him? Dom and Carrie-Anne?*

Justin could feel a slight tremble inside but what was really bugging him now was the plastic that was cutting into his wrists. They knew he wasn't a threat. In fact, they'd given him a job. Why couldn't he just get someone in here quickly and deal with the restraint on his wrists. He had a flight to book.

# Chapter 09

Kirsten watched from the roof as the gangster left the nightclub in a car with the blonde woman in tow. They stood beside the vehicle talking briefly, which allowed Kirsten time to run to the side of the roof and shimmy down onto the street outside. She took several looks from people in the side street, but Kirsten ignored them, checking around and locating a moped nearby. She jumped onto it, quickly broke into the ignition system, and started it up. As she drove off, she realised she had no helmet and hoped that the wig she was wearing wouldn't suddenly disappear off her head.

She watched as the car shot past her on a corner and she slowly picked up the tail from behind. Today she looked the part, backpack on, t-shirt, a tourist just out enjoying the open roads. The road wound up into local mountains behind the town. She thought mountains but they were more like hills, not having great height, but were very distinctly different to the town she just left.

As she rode along, she saw the car in the distance take a left up into what looked like an orange grove. Kirsten continued past it before then pulling off the road and hiding the bike under a small bush.

She got down low, running across the hillside as best she could before pulling out her binoculars and spying into the compound. There were a number of wooden buildings. Kirsten reckoned they must have been hot inside, as there were no air conditioning units around and the appearance of the sheds were simply like workhouses, places for storing tools and equipment used in the gathering of the orange plantation. Kirsten remained low down in the grass and watched as the gangster disappeared off in the car along with the blonde woman who seemingly approved to what she had seen.

Kirsten could have tailed them back, but she wanted to investigate this unit. For two hours, she lay down in the long grass, watching carefully until a van arrived. From the rear of it, a woman was taken out with a black hood over her and marched into one of the warehouses. The woman's hands were behind her back and had a plastic tie holding them tight.

Kirsten continued to watch the site, looking around at the various people. It seemed like a busy orange plantation. There were no guns in view but there were plenty of men lingering about. They didn't seem to be doing an awful lot of work and Kirsten could tell there were guns hidden within certain jeans and back pockets. At one point, some tourists came up asking about the grove and she could see them being fobbed off but in a polite way. She wondered if any of the police would show up, if they were in cahoots with the men in front of her.

On one occasion, several women turned up. They looked like women who could handle themselves, possibly part of the gang or terrorists or whoever these people were. She was struggling to fully understand what was going on, but she knew that this was a potential place that Craig could be.

At around about four o'clock in the afternoon, Kirsten decided that she would need to infiltrate the place at night, for in the daytime, the hillside was too open and she was struggling now to keep hidden, despite doing a recon from a distance.

Carefully, she worked her way back to the moped before driving it off to a different town and then commandeering a different bike. This one was a little bit more pepped up and Kirsten drove back to the cave, where she suited up in black as well as arming herself to a much higher degree. She hoped that no one was moved away in the time it would take her to get back but it was a risk she'd have to take, for going in as she was previously was not going to work.

Kirsten ate some cold beans from a tin before devouring some bread that she picked up on the way back. She would have liked to sit in a restaurant somewhere, eating something proper, but she didn't want to get spotted and have to go to ground. The last thing she needed was the heat of a police presence around where she was going to be. It was hot enough already.

As she went to exit the cave to perform a mission that night, her phone began to ring and she looked down, seeing it was Justin Chivers. She thought it was best to take the call, and find out what was happening.

'It's Kirsten. What's up, Justin?'

'Excuse the deception,' said a voice, 'but I had to get to speak to you directly. Mr Chivers didn't have an option in this, so I hope you'll forgive him.'

It was Godfrey. What did he want with her now? Why would he speak so direct?

'I wasn't looking to hear from a former employer,' said Kirsten.

'No, but you may need my help. It seems that things have got a little bit difficult for you in Zante. I believe the local authorities are looking for you and I believe you've lost Craig somewhere along the line.'

Kirsten was annoyed, but the man spoke like it was a minor imposition that was going on, rather than the idea that her lover could be dead.

'It's fine, it's under control. It's just about sorted out.'

'Really? Because I heard you were talking to Mr Chivers, trying to see if there was a certain angle involved. If that angle is correct, then I don't think this will be a simple issue.'

'I know where he is. Well, at least I've got a very good idea. When I return from there tonight, I'll either have Craig or I'll know where he is.'

'That may be the case, but I think there's more to it than just Craig.'

'What do you mean?' asked Kristen.

'You were asking about a Russian angle to Mr Chivers. The Huntress, the one who incapacitated your team and Anna had to capture. She was too dangerous to be allowed to be prisoner swapped.'

'So, what, you killed her?'

'Yes, you seemed to be rather astonished by the concept. It happens quite a lot, I'm afraid. Sometimes you have to protect yourself. Some people are just too good to be let out on their own. I had to protect everyone, you included.'

'Just lock her up,' said Kirsten. 'You could have just locked her up. You've got to tell me she has family.'

'She has family but I'm unsure of what's going on. I'd like to see this resolved properly though; therefore, I'd like to give you some assistance.'

'Did Anna Hunt come to you? Did Justin go to Anna Hunt and Anna Hunt come to you?'

'That's exactly what happened,' said Godfrey.

That hit Kirsten rather strangely. Godfrey giving up how he knew straight away. Also, it wasn't very Anna. Go and talk to Godfrey; get Godfrey to deal with it. No, that wasn't her at all. She wouldn't have been on to him. Anna, she'd been out here, she'd have been . . . It dawned on Kirsten that something was up.

'Where's Anna?' asked Kirsten.

'I said to Mr Chivers that you were good. I said that you would get involved in such a way that this whole thing could blow up. Anna Hunt was out investigating something for me in Greece, and she's now missing. I wish to get her back. I also wish to get back your Craig in one piece and you can go off and do whatever you want.'

'No, you don't. You're worried about Craig being taken by the Russians. You think there's Russian involvement in this as well.'

'Everything does point to Russian influence.'

'Which group of Russians though? The Russian authorities or Russians on the loose, like the Huntress was?'

'I don't know,' said Godfrey. 'That I'll tell you, and it's the truth. I am unaware of who's perpetrating this, but when I do, I will crush them. I will go for them, and I will make it clear that this won't happen again.'

'You want me to get Anna, don't you? That's why I'm here. Any of your people here as well?'

'Mr Chivers will be arriving.'

'What did you do? Jump him? Are you watching him much closer? He thought he was free within the service.'

'Nobody's free within the service,' said Godfrey. 'Not even me, not even Anna. Of course, we were watching him, and he gets a phone call from an outside source, someone of interest such as yourself, and he doesn't report it.'

'He was going to talk to Anna. He was going to find out for me what happened to the Huntress.'

'That's a topic that doesn't get brought up, a topic you will not bring up. I hope we understand each other on that.'

'I don't care what your secrets are. I want Craig back. Once Craig's back, I'm out.'

'And Anna? You wouldn't go and get Anna at the same time?'

'No,' said Kirsten, but she thought her tone unconvincing

'Justin will be over very soon. You can liaise through him to me. It's not a problem. If you need extra backup, let me know. End this and go your own way peacefully,' said Godfrey. 'Make a mess of it and bring everybody in and I'll have to take a much deeper interest.'

'You're interested already. You just think I'm the best person for the job out here, and you know I won't stop.'

'Very perceptive, Miss Stewart, and I hope you're right. I hope you do manage to solve this in the next couple of hours, but in case you don't, I'll be here.'

Kirsten saw the call close down and she made a mental note that Justin's number was compromised. He was also coming out. In one sense that did cheer Kirsten up, for the man was an operator. He knew how to get information. He could hack into the police services here, maybe even some intelligence services. He could operate out in the field as well like Dom and Carrie-Anne.

Kirsten tried to work out whether or not she should make sure the team knew about each other. Had Justin given up his information willingly, eagerly to the service? Had the service come to find it out from him? Godfrey said they had, at which point Justin probably made the call. It was better to work with than to work against. Maybe he didn't even have a choice.

Because she'd been disturbed, Kirsten rechecked her backpack, and then crawled out of the cave down onto the dark beach and walked over to the gentle waves pushing back and forward on the sand. She took a breath of sea air once, twice, a third time, calming herself, preparing herself for what was ahead. She knew when she infiltrated, they'd come for her, so she'd have to be smooth and she'd have to be able to find Craig quickly.

If they realised she was on scene, they may shoot him before she even saw him. She walked to where she'd hidden the bike nearby the cave. Kirsten thought about Anna Hunt. *Would she save Anna? Would she be there for her if it came to it? Probably,* she thought. That was the problem. Kirsten would find it hard to just walk away, but if she had Craig safe that might all change.

Pulling the bike out from underneath a tree at the roadside, Kirsten hopped on in her entirely black gear and drove off with no light on the front of the bike. She'd take the back roads as best she could which would mean a circuitous route round to the orange plantation, but at least she'd get there without anyone seeing where she'd come from.

As she rode along, the warm breeze on her face and her natural hair now blowing out behind, Kirsten gave thought to the next few hours. It was crunch time. She needed to find Craig and get him out. It was a moonlit night as well, not the best for sneaking about. She would rather have had wind and rain to drown out the sound and clouds to make everything as dark as possible. But this was summer on Zante, and things were very different.

76

# Chapter 10

Kirsten sat in the warm night, darkness all around, watching the dim lights of the compound. There was a light breeze, and she could hear the rustle of the trees. The hanging oranges were unseen, but the gentle swing of the branches was quite distinct in the night. There was minimal activity, and Kirsten waited until the hour had gone two o'clock before she made her move.

For the last two hours, there'd been the occasional guard patrolling every twenty minutes. He had no gun on show, was dressed in black and was hard to see, but he came out and he scoured the area with what looked like a pair of infrared binoculars. Kirsten was down low behind a boulder, and it seemed to work, for no one had approached her. After the man's last round at two o'clock, Kirsten moved out, quickly but silently, through the dry grass that surrounded the plantation.

A barbed wire fence was the first obstacle, but it wasn't electrified, and Kirsten found it easy to clamber up, then lay down a small blanket across the barbed wire, before rolling over and dropping down. She leaped up, pulling her blanket back off and tucking it away into the backpack she was wearing. She drew out a gun, silencer on it, and stared around the compound. As she crept closer to one of the huts, she heard a slight commotion which made her race to a hut, placing her back up against it and out of sight of the front of the huts.

She took out her mirror, checked around the corner and saw a group of men talking. The easiest thing to see was the end of the cigarettes, as they all seemed to be smoking hard, almost as if they were just getting the last drags in before they were going to do something. No guns were on show, but Kirsten knew they'd be there somewhere, hiding inside the jackets or the jeans of the men.

She spun round, went to the other side of the wooden hut she was at. There were five huts in total. Two vehicles were now positioned between the huts. She hadn't seen them earlier, but they had been here since she came back as no vehicles had arrived. They were minibuses and the windows looked as if they had been blacked out.

*Were they going to move people tonight?* She'd have to be quick. Voices came from the front of the huts, so Kirsten continued to the rearmost one, where, again, there was no one seemingly on guard. Maybe they were inside. She snuck up to the front door, realised it was secured with a padlock, so dipped into her clothing to take out her lock picks.

With a quick glance around, Kirsten saw there was no one in sight and quickly undid the lock. There was nothing sophisticated about it, and she had the lock open in five seconds. Lock picks now put back inside her clothing, she quietly slipped off the lock and left it on the floor before removing the latch of the door. With a last glance around her, she pushed it open.

A quick glance around told Kirsten that there were at least six people in there, but all were sitting down on benches. No one was standing. She closed the door behind her and quickly checked the women over, realising all of them had their hands behind their back with a plastic tie tying them tight. There was a hood over each of their heads, and Kirsten hadn't said anything. This made her realise that the people must be used to the idea that someone would come in to check on them.

Kirsten looked around for a light switch, saw one on the wall, and thought about switching it on. The problem was she wasn't sure if the light could be visible outside. There was no window in the hut, but it was wooden and would a shaft of light be seen? She couldn't risk it, so got close to the first person, who she realised was a woman.

She was large, and Kirsten undid the hood that was over her, lifting it off her head, and slapping a hand over the woman's mouth. The woman looked up at her, first in fear, and then with an excitement. Kirsten indicated that she should be quiet and slowly began to remove the hand from her mouth. The woman said something in Greek. Kirsten was unsure what it was, so she indicated for the woman to say it again. *Save me, something about save me,* thought Kirsten. She gave a quick nod to the woman and put a finger up across her mouth so the woman would stay quiet.

Kirsten knew she had to move and move quickly. She scanned the rest of the occupants of the room, and they were all women. Craig was not here. Kirsten returned to the door, pried it open, and placed a mirror outside. She could see someone had moved into one of the minibuses, but there was also some commotion between two figures beside the vehicles; one was pointing out to the perimeter. The man he was talking to seemed to be agitated. In his mouth was a large cigar. Kirsten watched as he pointed to the man who reported to him, indicating places along the perimeter.

Kirsten wondered at the man's abilities, for if there was someone out there, the last thing he wanted to do was to be seen, and he was standing with a cigar lit, the red end evident in the night. The other problem was that if someone was out there it could impede Kirsten's escape plan. As she sat looking through the mirror at the man, there was no noise until his head suddenly flew back, the cigar dropping from it. He clattered into the man behind him, falling to the ground motionless.

The man standing beside him almost went into shock and then threw himself to the ground. Once there he took out his gun and started firing off into the distance. This caused a cacophony of gunfire.

Kirsten closed the door quickly. She ran round the women, pulling off their headcover, looking at foreign faces until she grabbed the covering of the woman at the rear. Anna Hunt looked back up at her.

'What the hell?' said Kirsten.

'Just cut me loose. We're going to need to go.'

Kirsten thought for a moment. Anna was dangerous. They'd fallen out before Kirsten left the service, but if she was free, she could do a lot of damage, very, very quickly, to these people.

'I'm here for Craig. He's in here somewhere. I know it.'

'Fine,' said Anna, 'we need to get out. Now cut me loose.'

Kirsten took a knife from inside her jacket and cut Anna loose, before beginning on the rest of the women.

'Just leave them. They're just being held by the terrorists. They're not going to kill them. They'll ransom them.'

'They deserve a chance to get free, too,' said Kirsten quietly, under her breath, and she began to cut the women loose.

'They'll run out into that gunfire.'

It hadn't stopped. All around them, bullets were raining in, and Kirsten indicated to the women, once she'd cut them free, that they should stay down low. Anna was at the front door, peering out carefully.

'Do you have a gun?' she asked Kirsten. Kirsten reached inside her jacket, handing over a small handgun.

'Magazine?' Kirsten handed over the trim supply of bullets.

'There's buses out there,' said Anna. 'We could get on the bus and get out.'

'Get the back door open, and we can throw these women in,' said Kirsten.

'I meant you and me,' said Anna. 'We need to get out of here. This is not our fight.'

'They took Craig. It's my fight. I need to search the other buildings.'

'Fine,' said Anna, 'but we need to do it quick. Probably best to do it while there's this chaos going on.'

The door suddenly opened, and Kirsten saw Anna fire at point blank range, blood smattering her. Whoever it was that opened the door had obviously fallen away, but she closed it again briefly, before pushing it open and firing outside.

'Forget searching anything. We have to get out. There are people coming in.'

Kirsten yelled at the women to stand. 'We go for the back of the minibus,' said, Kirsten. 'You go out, and I'll hold the door. Chase the women out into the minibus.'

'So be it,' said Anna. She pushed the door open, running out, firing into the night. Kirsten placed herself at the door. It was hard to see, figures drifting here and there. So far, there was only one good figure, if you could call it that, and five other scared ones behind her in the hut. Kirsten dropped her gun hand and stepped back inside as the wood around her splintered.

'The door's open,' shouted Anna. Kirsten glanced to her right. The rear door of the minibus had indeed been opened, and Kirsten yelled at the woman beside her. She wasn't sure how much English they understood, but she shouted at her to run to the bus, grabbed her by the arm, pulled her out the door, and threw her in the general direction.

Anna Hunt was down on one knee from behind the bus, firing away, and began yelling at the women to get inside. Kirsten threw them out one by one firing covering rounds in between. As the last woman ran across, Kirsten saw her spin and fall to the ground. She stepped out, firing several times before picking the woman up, one arm underneath the woman's shoulder, and she dragged her quickly across to the bus, throwing her at it and telling the others to pull her inside.

'I'll get the wheel,' shouted Anna.

'I'll hold here,' said Kirsten, going down on one knee and quickly firing all around her. As she looked to the hut that was ahead of her, she saw a group of people being dragged out and a bus being pulled up in front. A pair of bare legs marched in front of her. The man had his hands tied up behind him and there was a hood over his head. He was wearing a white t-shirt with his underpants.

Kirsten looked at the figure. That was Craig. Dammit, that was Craig. She went to run towards him, but a hail of gunfire came in at the minibus. Kirsten rolled down underneath it, and she could hear the tires being shredded by gunfire. She rolled up onto the other side of the minibus, where she was at the passenger side, and banged on the window, shouting at

Anna Hunt to go. Kirsten pulled open the passenger door and jumped in as the vehicle started and went full tilt to the edge of one of the huts.

As it rounded the corner, another minibus was there, and they collided straight into it. Kirsten was thrown forward against the main door and then fell to the ground. As she rolled up, she yelled at the women to just get clear. She couldn't do any more for them. She was trapped now, in the middle of all this gunfire, with no way out.

'I'm going for Craig,' she shouted. 'I saw Craig.'

Anna Hunt nodded and tried to extricate herself from the vehicle. Kirsten ran around the back of the vehicle, towards the hut at the front, where she had seen the minibus that Craig had been thrown into. As she rounded the corner of another hut, looking at where the minibus should be, she noticed several disappearing down the road.

'Damn,' she yelled, before having to throw herself backwards behind one of the huts as more gunfire came in. She rolled out of the way, only into the feet of a man looking down at her. He held his gun to her, indicating she should get up. She looked at him, wondering how she could take him out. He suddenly fell backwards, bounced off the wall of the hut behind her, blood seeping out from his chest.

'This way,' said Anna. 'They've come for us.'

Kirsten followed Anna back to where their bus collision had taken place, then out towards the rear of the compound where the fence had been cut. She raced through it in the night, several figures in black surrounding them, all armed with heavy machine guns. As they got out into the surrounding scrubland, a figure turned to Anna, telling her she was safe now, but Anna asked him for a code. The man stopped in his tracks.

'You're with us now. You're safe. We have got you all clear.'

Anna Hunt looked at the man, sizing him up. 'What's my code?' she said.

The man looked at her, almost quizzically.

'What's my name?' asked Anna. Again, it was the same response. Kirsten watched Anna begin to raise her gun, but a second man, standing close to her, drove the butt of his rifle into her head. Kirsten went to react but felt a tip of a machine gun placed in the back of her neck.

'No, no, no. No, no, no,' I said. 'Be more careful of the white women.' Watch the white women, the women from the North, the women without the tan. They'll fetch a pretty price.'

Kirsten's hands were pulled behind her, the gun removed, and she felt them being bound together. A plastic tie cut into her wrists, so tight as it pulled. She was then pushed forward and walked a quarter of the mile in the dark, gunfire still behind them. Soon, they arrived at a car where Anna was dumped into the boot, still unconscious, having been dragged all the way there. Kirsten was forced into the back seat, a hood put over her.

'We go for a ride now. Time to meet the boss. Don't move and you'll be okay. Well, at least, until he meets you.'

Kirsten tried to breathe easy. It was not a time to panic. She couldn't see, her wrists were bound, and she wasn't going to do anything at this point. Better to get there, see her situation, and if Anna Hunt was with her, they'd be twice as likely to get out. Though she couldn't see because of the hood, the image of Craig himself, bound and head covered, flashed through her mind. She'd been so close. Were they still going to keep him alive, or were they going to do something else? Kirsten's stomach turned over.

# Chapter 11

Kirsten had been delivered a blow to the head at some point in the car. It was the last thing she remembered until she woke up. The first thing she was aware of was she was upside down. She still had a cover over her head, but her ankles were extremely sore. Her hands and arms were also aching. She was still tied up behind, the plastic cutting into her, but her arms weren't hanging down, instead, they were being held awkwardly up her back because she was upside down. It was, without doubt, one of the most uncomfortable positions she'd been in.

She'd been relieved of her backpack and of any weapons and though the air wasn't cool, she was aware that she had distinctly less clothing on than when she'd started the night's attack. She believed she was down to her underwear.

She could hear the occasional shuffling around her and even through the hood she wore, she could smell the smoke of cigarettes. Occasionally, someone would laugh, but Kirsten decided not to engage them in any type of conversation, instead trying to let them think that she was still out cold so she could better read the situation before she'd have to interact with it.

She wondered why she was taken like this. There clearly had been an attack on the compound beyond her activities. Someone else had wanted those women, at least somebody had wanted Anna Hunt. Did they know who Kirsten was? Maybe they did, but the men who had taken them hadn't seemed local. Kirsten wondered what sort of gang warfare she was getting into. It wasn't factions of terrorists. The whole situation was so muddy and unclear that she found it hard to think it through. Maybe that was because she was hanging upside down, feeling the pressure on her head. She could swing from her current position. She could even lift herself up, she thought, to where her restraints on her feet were but trying to break out of the bonds with her hands lashed behind her was the difficult bit.

There was a sudden tension in the room and the shuffling of people and the odd clinking of bottles which made Kirsten's stomach churn. It felt like somebody important had entered the room. There were words in Greek, quick, in an accent almost mumbled and Kirsten couldn't pick them up. Someone was there in front of her. She felt a hand run down, first her left leg and then her right, and then it ran across her backside before touching her in a place that only Craig ever got to touch. The hands continued to examine her body in a rough way before eventually the hood was pulled down off her face.

'Now, who are you?' said a voice. Suddenly, there was a face upside down in front of Kirsten. 'I compliment you on that body. Clearly, you work out. You'd make a lot of money doing other sorts of business than what you're in.'

Kirsten glanced to her side. Anna Hunt was hanging there in a similar predicament as herself, but she seemed to still be out cold. Kirsten saw Anna's hair hanging down and touching the floor.

'How do you know Anna?' asked the man. 'Hmm? How do you know? She was clearly working with you and clearly, you'd come for her.'

Kirsten said nothing. She didn't want the man to feel he had the upper hand, though quite clearly, he did. His hands rolled over her again in a fashion that she only let Craig do. Inside, a fire burned in her, and if she got out of these bonds, she would rip this man apart.

'Aren't you going to speak to me?' he said as he grasped her buttock. He was anything but delicate and Kirsten fought hard to maintain her silence. 'Such a pity to mark this body.'

The man stepped across to Anna Hunt and was handed a large bucket of water which he threw over her. It was clearly cold for Anna suddenly startled into life. 'Miss Hunt,' the man said, 'you'll be fetching a good price when they eventually come for you but first, you're going to tell me something, aren't you?' The man ran his hands over Anna's body in a similar fashion he'd done to Kirsten. Kirsten could see her anger. As the man got close to her, she spat in his face.

'No, no,' he said, 'we don't do that. You see I have the upper hand.' He ran his hands down the legs of Anna Hunt as he stood up again. As his hands went further down her body, reaching parts where only lovers should reach, Kirsten saw Anna's back begin to flex.

She suddenly swung herself up and planted her forehead with force between his legs. The man buckled backwards. For a moment, he bent down nursing himself before stepping forward and launching an almighty kick into the middle of Anna's stomach. Kirsten watched her struggle to breathe and spit before the man hit her with another couple of punches to the stomach and then down with one to the jaw.

'Beat them,' he said, 'Beat them, whip them, do whatever but I want some information from them before we move them on.' He turned and walked out the door leaving the two women hanging there as his team watched them closely.

The next four hours were some of the worst of Kirsten's life. At first, they tried to physically beat her. Then she was abused before she was beaten again. She told them nothing and neither did Anna and by the time the men had left them, still hanging in that same position, Kirsten was sore all over and physically feeling sick at where the men's hands had been.

'Your first time like this?' asked Anna, blood weeping out from the side of her face.

'You should know, you were my boss.'

'True, it's not my first time. See all that anger you've got, the one that wants to rip every head off the body of those men, store it, get ready to use it.'

'I need to find Craig. Why are they coming for you? Why are they coming for him? What's going on?'

'Craig shot Control,' said Anna very plainly. 'Craig killed Control. They're coming for him for that.'

'Who's coming for him?'

'The Russians.'

'But that was ages ago. Why come for him for that? She was undercover. There's no reason to go tit-for-tat on that. We didn't do the dirty; she was. She was smack in the middle of our organisation and she got caught out. No, spies don't work like that. Otherwise, we'd be shooting each other left, right, and centre; there'd be no end to it.'

'But then her sister came for her,' said Anna.

'And we captured her.' Kirsten saw the look from Anna. 'Well, you did. You took her to Godfrey. Paid a heavy price for it, too.'

'Dom and Carrie-Anne got out alive, off enjoying themselves now. Justin was okay; he recovered. You recovered before you left us.'

'But why come to kill us? Kill you? Kill Craig? We've still got the Huntress. Who on earth is going to come like this? We could just dispatch her.'

Kirsten saw Anna's face, the woman wincing for a moment and then she smiled over at Kirsten. 'One of the things about working for us is you don't get to know everything. Decisions are made. Important decisions, decisions you can be no part of.'

'You made a decision. You made a decision that's impacting Craig?'

'No,' said Anna, 'Godfrey did. A decision that's impacting me as well. Look at me, we have to get out because if we don't, we're going to go to the Russians. I came over here tailing someone, and then following up a lead, but it was all false. It was just to get me, but it was clever because they never sent the Russians after me. Instead, the local gangsters have set this thing up with a bit of help. I didn't see it coming. Now they have me and they'll exchange me. That's why we're not dead. That's why they took us out, but I don't think the local gangsters know who you are, but they soon will. You'll get traded over as well.'

'But they're coming for us because of a decision. What happened?' asked Kirsten, 'Tell me what happened.'

'Godfrey did a little exchange. Our man came out, he's tucked away somewhere. The Huntress got on a plane and Godfrey blew it up over the water.'

'Why?'

'He couldn't let somebody like her go loose,' said Anna; 'she's too dangerous. That sort of vengeance, it wasn't going to stay there. It wasn't sated. It would come back. We got lucky. You got lucky, if I hadn't showed up, if I hadn't . . . you'd have lost them, all of them.'

'It's you that got me into it in the first place.'

'Don't start that,' said Anna, suddenly choking. She spat out some blood. 'You're not innocent in all this; you tracked Control down. Craig killed her.'

'Just doing our job.'

'And Godfrey was just doing his. He's spot on. She could have come back, taken out many of us, could've wreaked havoc on us. I would've killed her as well. That's what you miss, that instinct, that brutal instinct.'

'I'm getting kind of fed up with people telling me what I'm not,' said Kirsten. Her throat was parched. When they'd beaten her, she'd sweated in this room, wherever it was. She could feel the lacerations across her back where they'd put a whip to her, but the physical beating she could endure but some of the other abuses were racing back to her mind now.

'Suck it in, let it back out when you get a chance,' said Anna.

Kirsten looked away from her scanning the room around, but she could see no help. Her head was pounding, no doubt from being upside down for so long.

'We need to get out,' said Anna. 'If they get us to the Russians, we're dead, worse than dead. This will be nothing to what they'd do to us. We killed one of their own. Well, technically Craig did. They'll see it as you and me that did it. Certainly, me that did for her sister. That's the trouble. Where's professionalism these days? More like gangsters. In the old days, nothing would've been said, all quiet. Maybe one day they'd have grabbed you, ended you.'

'So, Godfrey finished somebody off and now Craig's disappeared. It was different working for Macleod, you do realise that? There was a standard where you're held up to.'

'Oh, give over,' said Anna. 'That was the police; this is different. This is about getting the right thing for the country, defending it at all costs. It's not about some sort of idea of law enforcement and you joined it. Nobody forced you, not even Macleod, but he was right, you were good at it. I don't know what you're going to do now. You've seen too much, and it all stays with you. You don't go back to being a police officer. You can't join him again.'

Kirsten knew that was true. The first reaction these days was to manhandle someone for now she worked outside the law. Craig had disappeared and she hadn't turned to the police. She had gone off to handle it herself. Although in fairness, a number of people had come after her.

The door opened and the same man who had initially come in and ordered their beatings now came and stood between the two of them. He ran his hand down the outside leg of both women.

'Such a pity to damage such lovely property. This one's too old,' he said, pointing to Anna Hunt. 'But you, I could have taken you back, let you live in my bedroom. Had a few years of enjoying you before letting you out somewhere. But Miss Kirsten Stewart, it appears that you're wanted, too. You're going to be exchanged so we need to clean you up. Miss Hunt here can wait. I have a bigger buyer for her.' Kirsten didn't understand what it meant, but as the man walked away, she saw one of his cohorts who had entered the room attaching a hose to a tap. As she hung there, she was hosed down before she was scrubbed, suds all over her face and the rest of her body. Once they'd hosed her down again, the water dripping off her, making her feel so cold, someone walked up, smacked her across the head, causing her to black out. The last word she heard was Anna whispering across to her, 'Pick your time.' The same words came back to her as she heard the car engine turning over.

# Chapter 12

Kirsten's head was once again covered, but she could smell the cigarette smoke and the musky scent of the man beside her. He may have been the one who had previously beaten her or washed her, but either way, she didn't care. Anna Hunt had said it—she needed to be ready. One thing that was bothering Kirsten was the fact that she was going to a different buyer than Anna Hunt. Maybe the Russians hadn't got on to her yet, or maybe they didn't realise that the people who had taken her had her. Clearly, someone else had.

Kirsten was finding this game very hard because she didn't know all the players. The car bounced along the road and Kirsten felt the wind coming in through the window. They clearly hadn't dressed her again, as she was still in her underwear, hands still strapped up behind her back. The smell of the sea was prevalent as they drove along, so she must have been near the coast. That was a pleasant smell. It was only the musky scent of the man and a cigarette smoke that turned it more putrid. She was sore, her arms aching, and her back screamed from where she'd been whipped.

She knew she'd have to get those wounds treated but right

now she needed to survive the next half an hour or whenever it was they brought her to an exchange point. Her head was still pounding possibly from being hung up for so long, but also from the fact that they hadn't dried her down after pouring cold water all over and cleaning her up.

The suds had hurt and they'd gone into her wounds from the beating, but at least she knew the infections probably would be stayed. That's why they were doing it at the end of the day. The last thing they needed to do was hand over goods that were going to die first.

Kirsten steeled herself from what was about to come. The car pulled up and the man beside her leaned over closer, and she felt a hand run down her arms as he checked her bindings behind her.

'The boss is right; would've been good seeing you around for a while.'

The man's English was good and Kirsten wondered why his boss hadn't used him to speak to her before. The interrogation questions had come from another great man whose voice was a lot higher. Still, it didn't matter, if she got the chance she'd lay waste to the lot of them, but only if Craig didn't get them first.

The thought jumped into her mind without her thinking. Yes, her man would've defended her if he was there, but he wasn't, he had disappeared. That's why she was in this situation. All she wanted was to get him back, get him back and get out. Anna, Godfrey, and the rest could just go.

She had a moment as she thought about Dom and Carrie-Anne coming into the situation. Would they end up where she was? They've been part of the team after all that had been involved with the Huntress, but Kirsten couldn't worry about that now. She had to get away. She needed to wait for that moment.

The man beside her got out of his side of the car and she heard the door shut before her own car door was opened and she was pulled out. The hood was ripped off her head in an unceremonious fashion and the bright light of the sun forced her to squint. She was dragged by her biceps, one man on each arm, and then she tried to look around.

She realised that she was on the edge of a small ravine where a river ran down below and there was a small wooden bridge across it. Kirsten and her captors were on one side. On the other side, she saw at least three men dressed in an array of shirts and trousers, all with sunglasses on, some with hats protecting themselves from the heat of the sun. She guessed it must have been about the middle of the day as the sun was high.

Kirsten was led slowly over to the bridge. She was then told to stop on the edge. A gun was placed on her back, and she was advised not to move, but the man who had spoken such good English made his way to the centre of the bridge to be joined by one of the men from the other side. The other man had a case, and as they got close to the edge, they stopped just short of each other. Something was said in Greek and the case was left down on the bridge, while the two men returned to Kirsten's side.

The man from the other side put his hand up to Kirsten's face, turned her head this way and that, looking at her. He examined her eyes, then checked the wounds around her body, pushing the fingers into the grooves where she'd been whipped, causing her to wince.

'She's a bit banged up,' Kirsten heard him say in Greek. There was a reply that she thought was some sort of swearing. Then there was a coming together of the pair, something about the deal being on. They walked back to the middle of the bridge where the original captor picked up the briefcase, opened it and began counting the money.

No one moved while he did so, and the hot sun beat down on Kirsten. She looked around scanning into the hills, wondering if she could do anything. She leaned over, looking down into the river off the bridge, but a gun was pressed up against her.

'No, you don't. When he's finished counting the money,' said the new captor, 'you'll be coming with me to the far side of the bridge. Once there, I'll explain the rest. Don't try to move.'

There was clearly little trust between the men for the money was counted fully. Kirsten stood, feeling the sun beating down upon her breastbone, sweat running off her face, dripping down onto her skin. She didn't mind the sun normally, but that was when she chose to be there, chose to have a drink whenever she wanted. Now she was dehydrated, her head banged relentlessly, and she could feel the moment slipping away. With a gun at her back, there was no opportunity to escape.

Kirsten watched the original captor close the briefcase, stand up, and then shake hands with his opposite number. He turned, walked away while Kirsten was marched across the bridge. She was then turned so she could see the original captors get into the car and drive off. Kirsten was forced to stand there for the next couple of minutes until the car disappeared along the road and out of sight.

'Kirsten Stewart,' said her new captor, 'I see they tried to work some information out of you. Clearly didn't work. However, I'm not looking for information. You should know that the Russians have contacted me. They're prepared to pay me a good price, much more than what I've just handed over there. They said you're very dangerous.' He started to walk around her, and she could feel his eyes looking over.

'It's a pity you're so dangerous. I would have liked to have had my fun with you, first of all, but when they say someone is dangerous, you get worried. They said to me they didn't care if you were dead or alive, said to me I could just drop you off in a body bag and they wouldn't care. It makes me wonder what you did to them. You must have been good. I was quite lucky because it appears your previous captors didn't know exactly who you were. Your name has been circulating for a while. There's also another man, but I'm afraid that's going to be the end of your journey. You see, I don't take risks, and I'm certainly not keeping someone like you alive.'

Kirsten watched the other two men reach into the boot of the car and then bring a large blanket over. It was laid on the ground at the edge of the bridge, and the corners of it hung up on the supports, so it was like a large L shape. The man told Kirsten to stand on it. She did so, looking around, wondering how she would get out of this.

'We don't like to leave a mess at the scene,' he said, 'so if you don't mind.'

The man walked up to her and took out a small knife. He reached over, grabbing Kirsten's pants, cutting through one side and then the other, removing them from her. He then reached up and cut off the straps of her bra, removing it as well, leaving her completely exposed.

'Kneel down,' he said. 'Don't worry, I'm not going to do anything of a sexual nature, but if you kneel down, we'll catch any extraneous material once I shoot you. I don't want people to know where it ended.'

Kirsten remained standing.

'It's up to you,' he said. 'I can beat you down, leave you lying there while I shoot you, or you can kneel down with your back to me, you won't see it coming, and it will be over quick. I'm not unkind.'

Kirsten turned, believing if she could make the man think she was complying, there might be an opportunity to come. She knelt down on the large piece of white material.  The stones and the path underneath came up through, hurting her knees. He pushed her forward gently removing her shoes and tossed them to one side.

'My apologies,' he said. 'You really are quite something.'

She could hear him screwing in the silencer of the gun, and looking left and right, she saw she was flanked. The other two men held guns pointed towards her. Her stomach began to knot tight. She could feel her body physically shaking. Most of her do-or-die situations, it was all instinct, she just reacted. She didn't even have time to think about the fact she may not walk out of the situation but here she couldn't see anything. No way out. This was how it was going to end for her.

Her mind flashed back to the police force. Macleod, Hope, Ross, good days. She remembered stopping the assassination of the First Minister. The time on the train when she prevented London being bombed. She had done some good things, but this wasn't the time to stop. Her brother came to mind, and she felt her body begin to shake.

'There's no need to be embarrassed. It's okay to feel nervous at your death especially when it's coming like this,' said the man. 'It will just be a moment. I can hear a car in the distance.'

Kirsten could hear it too, coming closer to some nearby road and suddenly she felt there might be hope. Maybe a stay of execution, but then the car began to drift away again until finally it was gone.

'Good,' said the man. 'Goodbye, Kirsten Stewart. I'll make it as . . .'

Three shots rang out in quick succession and Kirsten jumped. Another three followed and she heard people falling to the ground beside her. She looked around and those who had flanked her were lying on the ground with two bullets gone through each head. She turned on her knees, the stones still pressing in and saw that her new captor was now lying on the ground, the gun away from his hand.

She stood up quickly, pushing herself up from her knees and looked around for somewhere to go. She didn't know what had happened, but she didn't know that anybody coming would be benevolent either. Maybe the Russians had double-crossed them. She quickly ran over to the car of her new captors, hiding down behind it and trying to scrape her hands against the wheel arch, seeing if she could snap the plastic bond. She heard footsteps approaching and braced herself to try and kick out whoever was there.

'Easy,' said a voice. Kirsten's heart lit up. 'Carrie-Anne, get something on her.'

It was Dom's voice, but the first person she saw was Carrie-Anne taking off her light jacket and wrapping it around Kirsten. 'Come on,' she said, helping Kirsten to stand. She took out a small knife, cut Kirsten's bonds, put an arm around her, and together the three of them walked off of the hill, away from the bridge.

'The car is just up beyond here. We'll get you in and we'll get somewhere safe. We've got you,' said Dom. 'We've got you.'

Kirsten drove her feet as best she could over the ground. Her shoes were back near the bridge, but they didn't wait to pick them up. Instead, she went across the gravelly ground until they found the car. When they reached it, Carrie-Anne helped Kirsten inside and got into the backseat with her while Dom started up the engine. He drove off, still saying the same words. 'We've got you, we've got you.'

Carrie-Anne said nothing. Instead, she wrapped her arms around Kirsten, holding her close and Kirsten laid her head into Carrie-Anne's shoulder. All of a sudden, the tears came. 'They've got Craig. I would've . . .'

'Shh,' said Carrie-Anne. 'It's okay. It's okay. Dom, move it.'

Kirsten lay sobbing as the car sped off along the dusty track. She had no way of knowing where she was going, but she was safe now. Dom and Carrie-Anne had come. They'd found her. She didn't know how, she didn't know why, but she didn't care. Kirsten Stewart was still alive.

# Chapter 13

The car pulled up in front of a small shack, some distance from the main town. Kirsten, led by Carrie-Anne with the coat still wrapped around her, hobbled inside, and found that the interior was far more palatial than the exterior would suggest. All modern conveniences were there from a well-stocked kitchen through to an electric shower, and a television and sound system in the front room. There were two bedrooms. Carrie-Anne first led Kirsten through to one bedroom, sitting her down on the bed before coming in with a towel and exchanging the coat for the towel.

Suitably wrapped up, Carrie-Anne then led her to the shower which started running, and placed Kirsten inside and told her to let the water soak her for at least ten minutes. Kirsten could hear Dom and Carrie-Anne talking outside, but at one point felt like she should say to them that she could hear.

'She's really taking it bad this time, and not in a good way,' Dom said.

'I know,' said Carrie-Anne. 'We've got to check those wounds over as well. Just let her soak for the minute; when she comes out, we'll dry her down. We'll set her up on the bed and you can tend to the wounds. You're better at that than I am.'

Kirsten stood in the shower, the water running down her, the occasional patch of blood within it. The last forty-eight hours had been like hell and she'd gone through torture, which she'd always been prepared for when she'd gone into the service. They even ran a course in it, but she'd never suffered like this at the hands of anyone.

When Carrie-Anne came back in after twenty minutes, Kirsten nodded when she asked if she'd shut off the shower and Carrie-Anne placed the towel around her, drying her ever so carefully while Kirsten stood. Once Carrie-Anne had finished, she took a fresh towel and wrapped it around Kirsten, taking the previous one which had signs of blood on it and dropping it into a laundry basket.

'I'm going to take you through to the bedroom. You lie down on your front. I'll put a towel over the other parts of you, but Dom's going to need to work on that back. I take it they whipped you.'

Kirsten nodded. She didn't feel like speaking. As she lay there, tears began again. She felt Carrie-Anne's hand passing through her hair.

'It's all right, love. It's okay; you can cry. You don't have to put on a show for us. Dom's cried in my arms before. It's not something that goes away. It's something you're going to need help with. He still needs help.'

There was a knock at the door and Dom entered the room, carrying a small bag.

'These are just my essentials. They should help clean you up, but I'll be able to assess if we need anything else; just lie still. I'll make sure that each wound's clean. Nothing looks beyond repair, but you will have some scars.'

Kirsten, with her face side on to the bed, let her eyes roam around to see Dom behind her. The man dropped to his knees and started cleaning her wounds out with something that stung. Every now and again she'd jump as a little pang of pain shot along her. She felt Dom's hands moving across, and at times she would shiver from it.

'Sorry,' he said, 'it brings it back, I know. I'm trying to be as medical about it as I can, so you don't feel . . . well, you know.'

'Just get it done,' said Kirsten. 'Get it done. I'll get some clothes on and we can talk.'

'Of course,' said Carrie-Anne, and Kirsten saw her give a nod to Dom, an encouragement to get on with it.

'I saw Anna. Anna Hunt was there.'

Dom stopped what he was doing and got chided by Carrie-Anne for it.

'Not now, Dom,' she said. 'Get finished with the wounds, then we'll sit inside. I'll get a cup of tea or something on for her. Okay?' Carrie-Anne went to leave the room but Kirsten stopped her.

'Don't. I know it's only Dom, but don't. Just stay here. It's just that he's . . . well, that's where they ran their hands, too.'

'Of course,' said Carrie-Anne. She knelt down in front of Kirsten's face and began rubbing her hand through her hair again. 'Whatever it takes, whatever we need. Okay?' She kissed the top of Kirsten's forehead.

An hour later, Kirsten was in the living room, wrapped up in a dressing gown Carrie-Anne had given her. In her hand was a hot cup of tea and she knew it was an obvious statement that a cup of tea helped everything, but she never realised just how true it was. It had taken her a while to steady her hand before she could drink the tea, but once the hot liquid was inside her, she started slowly to feel more like herself. It wasn't that what had happened had gone away, not by any stretch of the imagination and she believed Carrie-Anne when she said she would carry it for the rest of her life.

'Probably best not to think about it,' said Dom. 'When it happened to me, it took a long time to recover.'

'What happened?' asked Kristen.

'Foreign job, jumped on by a large number of men, very similar to yourself.'

Dom stopped short there and Carrie-Anne held up her hand to Kirsten. 'Now's not the time. You mentioned Anna Hunt and we've got Craig to think of. I know you're in no condition, but we need to start moving. You need to go operational here. You really need to push everything to one side.'

Kirsten nodded. Of course, she knew that's what she had to do, but doing it was something else. Anna had said to take the anger and she found herself doing that, driving it inside and forcing herself to think, to act like she'd just taken a simple beating.

'Anna was with you,' said Dom. 'What do you know about it?'

'Well, the ones who'd captured me first, they said that basically, someone was paying money for me, but the second captor said that the first ones didn't know who I was. They mentioned the involvement of Russians. Anna also told me that the Huntress, the one that nearly took the whole team out, Godfrey killed her—sent her back in a plane, and then took out the plane. He might have something to do with it, or it might just be the Russians. I don't know when the initial attack happened, and Craig was taken. They killed the mayor, and it was locals that were doing it. Then they hunted me down. I'm . . . I'm unsure what's going on. I don't know if there's a deal between them or what. I don't under . . .'

Tears started to stream down Kirsten's eyes, the frustration inside overwhelming her. Carrie-Anne leaned over close, pulling her tight.

'It's okay. We don't understand, that's okay. We're going to understand. Dom and I will go out into the town, shake a few things down, find out what's happening. You're going to lie here and try and get some sleep. Let those wounds heal a little. We'll come back with our intel, and we'll work out a plan of action. The next stage of this is on me and Dom, you understand?'

Kirsten nodded. She didn't have the strength at that point to get up and take charge.

'Thank you for coming. How did you . . . how did you even find me?'

'We arrived not long before the whole shootout. Dom clocked it on a police radio. We raced up to the scene; we saw people disappearing and being killed here, there, and everywhere. We couldn't get in to you after they took you, but we knew somebody was in there, for there was only two of you that went there. All the other women were taken elsewhere. It was heavily fortified, so then we tailed you. We had no idea Anna was with you.

'They set up the meet; it took us time to get into position and that's when we took them out. We waited until the other ones were gone because we weren't of the belief that we could take out six people at once. Two of us, three people, yes, but not six. Too risky, you could have died. So sorry we left you in such a horrible position.'

'You saved me,' said Kirsten. 'You saved me. It's fine. Just let me go to sleep.'

Kirsten lay down and the last thing she saw was her two compatriots leaving the house, and she heard the car disappear. Part of her wondered if she should have gone with them, protecting herself, but she trusted Dom and Carrie-Anne, that this would be a safe house away from anyone, that people wouldn't know she was here. If they had any belief that they did, they never would've left her. She turned over and tried to go to sleep, tried to ignore the sound in the back of her head, of the whip striking time and again.

Scene Break. Scene Break. Scene Break.

Dom sat at the bar, a large white hat on his head, in a white suit and looking like a cross between a mafia don and some old geezer sat out on a Spanish homestead. He was chatting to a lively young woman behind the bar and trying to ignore the attentions of another woman who was offering her wares to him. He had spoken to her briefly earlier, and she had nothing to offer in terms of what was happening within the town. However, the young woman behind the bar was much more forthcoming, especially when Dom kept on offering to buy her a drink at the same time.

'It's just got silly. I came over here from England for a quiet life, the bar, sunshine. What more do you want? Suddenly they're having this terrorist issue. I mean these are beach resorts. Why do they need terrorism?'

'Truth,' said Dom. 'Why indeed?' and went to clink his bottle of beer on hers.

'The way I see it is this is the terrorists flexing their muscles and the police need to get on top of them. That's, of course, if the police are even bothered about them; half the police force could be in it for all we know. They're just not happy with the mainland. Independence for the islands—can you imagine it? Wasn't that long ago, the country was struggling within Europe, needing help because of the monetary situation.'

'There's been a number of incidents, haven't there?'

'All the papers reported a number of things. The one I know about is the one on the beach,' said the woman. 'You see, the local mayor was down there; he'd organised a photo shoot on the beach. Apparently, they came in and knifed him. Some bodyguard or something tried to help and got taken away. They're saying around here, it's for extortion. They're looking for a bidder to buy him, so to speak. Didn't quite understand that. I don't know if I just . . . I don't understand the word for ransom correctly, but it was definitely to buy him. That just seems a bit mad doesn't it? Still, I wouldn't want it to put people like you off living around here,' said the girl.

'Well, I'm having a look, you know. Do you own this place?' asked Dom.

'No,' said the girl. 'I would love to, though.'

'I'd like my own as well down on the beach, you'd sit at my beach bar. The Beach Bum we could call it.'

The girl smiled back at him. 'Really? I always wanted that.'

'You on my arm, we'd go for it on a bar together, out on the beach, bikinis and Hawaiian shirts here, there, and everywhere.'

'Well, you'd suit the Hawaiian shirt,' she said.

Dom gave a smile, 'And so would you.'

The girl looked at him. 'I thought you'd want me in a bikini.'

'I'd want you the way you want to be,' he said. 'You look good behind a bar though. Must be plenty of guys give you a smile, keen to be served by you, but I don't know with the way the place is; what else has happened?'

'There's reports of other foreigners being taken. By the sounds of it some of them have been dumped back out again. It's almost like they didn't want them all of a sudden.'

*People hunting,* thought Dom, *not quite sure what Craig, Anna, and Kirsten really look like. Sounds like somebody's got the locals to do their work and their locals aren't particularly up to it.*

'When did this all kick off?' asked Dom. 'I mean, is it a short-term thing?'

'Probably two months ago. That's when it really started to get hyped up. Before that, they were painting slogans on walls, putting out posters generally just, you know, shouting a lot, not doing anything. It's all turned a bit nasty. The thing is the police don't seem to be acting on it, but then they're not like police we have back home. I think there's a lot of corruption going on.'

'Do you know that for sure?'

'No, but maybe they're scared. Maybe they're under pressure. Who knows? It hasn't been affecting the tourists though. I mean they don't go after the tourists so to speak. Just specific people, by the looks of it, but it's making people wary. Have you ever thought of the Caribbean?' she asked.

'Caribbean?'

'Yeah. Set up a bar in the Caribbean. I know how to run one. Maybe we should talk a little bit more on it.'

'Maybe,' said Dom, 'but I need to go now, but I'll be back. Trust me, I'll be back.' He went to push his beer bottle over to her, but she stepped around from behind the bar, strolled up to him and kissed him on the lips before stepping back.

'Make sure you do,' she said and turned and walked back to her position. Dom smiled, gave a tap of his hat, and walked out of the bar, hoping that Carrie-Anne wasn't inside. He took a glance around, but she must have been outside.

# Chapter 14

'Where have we got to?' asked Dom.

'I've been around every policeman in this bloody town,' said Carrie-Anne, 'every single one of them. Short of actually sleeping with them, they tell you nothing, and I'm not going that far.'

'Glad to hear it,' said Dom.

'At least not yet,' said Carrie-Anne. She saw Dom raise his eyebrows. 'We got a life on the line here, too,' she said; 'all options are on the table.'

He held his face, maintaining a pose that gave a nod of professional respect, but inside, he was angry. She didn't have to do that sort of thing. 'Have you found the big cheese yet?'

'Oh yeah, he's in there, and he liked me, too.'

'Why don't we go for it then?' said Dom.

'What do you mean?'

'Go for it. Go in, do the old tourist thing. Don't recognise who he is. End up taking him to bed and I'll be there in the room to make sure he gets talked to before any action happens.'

'Not a bit risky?' asked Carrie-Anne. 'What if he suggests going to his place?'

'Be persuasive,' said Dom. 'You know how to be persuasive.'

'You know though I can operate in the field, it's not natural to me. I'm more of an analyst, more a strategy person.'

'I know exactly what you are,' said Dom, 'that's why I wanted you to come with me. Craig's in trouble, Kirsten's a mess. We're going to have to take some risks here. I think this is going to be one of them.'

Carrie-Anne nodded and adjusted the dress she was wearing. A little bit more cleavage, more leg.

'Do I look the type yet?'

Dom shook his head. 'No, you don't,' he said. 'Come on, loosen up a lot more. Give it the old, 'I'm totally pissed' look. Let's put a ring on that finger.'

'Divorcee?' she said. 'Play the old divorcee?'

'Yes, over here. First time holiday away. Lost the girls. Give him a bit of a sob story as well, then give him the idea he's going to get his leg over. You can sell that.'

'Well, thanks very much,' said Carrie-Anne.

'Because you can act it well,' said Dom. 'Now take care. I'll get a room in the hotel opposite. I'll slip you the key later on in the evening, then you take him back there.'

'Okay,' said Carrie-Anne. She looked nervous so Dom reached over and gave her a kiss.

'You can do it because you're good at this.'

He watched her leave, walking back over to the bar they'd been in earlier, but as soon as she was out of sight, he made his way to the hotel opposite. Once inside, he sorted himself a room, took the key upstairs and checked out the facility to make sure it was enough. There was no way to look into the room if he closed the curtains; the room was secure in that sense. He could stand in a small alcove then, as soon as the door was opened, step out, have a gun at the man's head without even thinking about it. Everything looked good.

Dom locked the room with the old-fashioned key he'd been given and then entered the bar opposite on the other side of the street. He sat in the corner nursing a beer for the evening, his eyes watching, making sure Carrie-Anne would be okay. It seemed to him that the small group of police that were there were certainly having a good time. A number of different women came and went, and they seemed to be trying it on.

Carrie-Anne had made a beeline for the police chief. He got up and started dancing for some reason, and she joined him in some embarrassing effort. Clearly, he liked the idea that she seemed completely drunk. The next thing she was sitting on his lap talking. Dom watched as his hand went round her hip and made its way up her back and the next thing, they were kissing. At this point Dom quietly brushed past them, slipping the room key to Carrie-Anne's open palm.

Champagne was brought out, and other wine. Dom watched Carrie-Anne knocking it back. She could hold her drink well, but there was an awful lot going down. He left the bar at about half past one in the morning and stood on the other side of the street in the shadows.

About half past two, Carrie-Anne emerged with the police chief. Dom made his way round to the back of the hotel, entering by the rear. He quickly strode up the stairs to the bedroom he'd sourced before, opened it with his lock picks and then closed it from inside. He stepped quietly into the alcove, gun at the ready.

The door opened to laughter and Carrie-Anne almost fell through. Dom saw the police chief give her backside a quick smack before encouraging her to get into the room. The big man closed the door behind him, stepped forward and Dom saw him reach for his belt. The dirty swine was going to go straight into action. Dom let him undo the belt, watched the trousers drop to his ankles before putting the gun at his head. If the man tried to move quickly, he'd fall over.

'Nice of you to join us. I'd like a little word with you. Don't turn round,' said Dom. He reached inside a pocket and pulled out a bag, and he then put it over the police chief's head. He walked him slowly, the trousers still down round his ankles, and sat him on a seat, pulling his arms behind him and tying his wrists together.

'This doesn't need to go badly for you. You're a man in a good position in this town, a man who knows things. I just want some information and a little help.'

'You know I'm the police chief,' he said. 'You know . . .'

The man's English was good. Dom pushed the gun to his head. 'And you don't know who I am, where I'm from, and what I want. I suggest you shut up and listen until I ask you to talk because a man with influence will know how to get himself out of this situation. A man without influence is going to be no use to me.'

The man went silent, and Dom looked over at Carrie-Anne who was giving him a large smile. *Oh, heck, she really is drunk, wasn't she?* 'What's the deal with the terrorists?' he asked.

'We have terrorists. One minute they're putting slogans up, the next they're kidnapping people, kidnapping tourists, trying to panic people,' said the police chief. He then hiccupped and belched. Apparently, the drink was getting to him as well.

'That's not what I mean. What's the deal with them? I've seen them. They seem to have got very good very quickly.'

'They are dealing with someone else,' he said. 'There are terrorist factions, lots of different ones. They're all fighting over each other. Suddenly they started kidnapping everyone. All these tourists. There were names out for people. Then they would kidnap some and then leave some. They were hiding them out of town. We know they're in some of the plantations around, but we have to be careful. You can't go rushing in; we haven't got the firepower. I don't have the people to go into that sort of thing.'

'What about the mayor?'

'The mayor had always been a pain to those terrorists, a right royal pain, you say, no. It's not surprising he got taken out, but then they kidnapped that man as well.'

'And what are you guys doing?'

'Keeping my head down. There are so many factions within these terrorists, it's hard to work out who's who. I just have people from the government complaining at me and telling me this and that. I run a police unit in this town, not for terrorists, for small crime, people doing a bit of drugs here and there. I'm not taking on people with guns.'

'Did they always have guns?' asked Dom.

'No, someone is supplying them and it's heavy weapons. It's not even a pistol or a handgun,' said the man, looking for the word. 'It's heavy weapons. They're planning on blowing things up. Suddenly, they get very serious, but their issue is not with us; they don't come after us. They go after civic things.'

Dom leaned closer to the man. He thought he could smell the man's fear. He was clearly sweating although that may have been just from having too much alcohol and the heat of the hotel room. Carrie-Anne certainly looked flushed.

'Do you know any of them, the leaders of these terrorist groups?'

'Some,' said the man.

'Do you know the one who was most likely to have taken the man who intervened with regards to the mayor?'

'Oh, I think so,' he said, 'Cortez. It's Cortez.'

'Are you sure it's him?'

'That's what the word on the street says but the word on the street can be wrong. I just know that Cortez is involved.'

'And how well does Cortez know you? Because I want you to set up a meet between me and Cortez.'

'Hang on,' said the man too loudly for Dom's liking. He slapped a hand over his mouth.

'You speak quietly. You speak quietly or you speak no more,' said Dom, pressing the handgun into the back of the man's neck. There was a quick nod.

'Hang on,' he whispered. 'That's the sort of thing that can get a police chief killed.'

'I'm only asking for an introduction, something simple, a meet. You don't have to tell him that I'm anything. You don't have to recommend me. Tell him exactly what's happened. You've got a gun at your head, so ask him to meet me. All he can do is say no. If he says no, however, I'll meet him in a very unfriendly way,' said Dom. 'At the moment I need to talk business. Do you understand me?' The police chief nodded. 'Good,' said Dom. 'I'll expect the meeting soon. Tomorrow night or the night after, but tomorrow night would be better. Somewhere simple, I don't mind if it's not open, but just let him know that I have my ways and means too; we'll be watched.'

The police chief nodded profusely. 'Now, will you let me go?' he said.

'You set up the meet, you and I are done. Not a problem. You don't set up the meet, and next time I'll actually pull the trigger.'

He watched the man start slightly before nodding his head quickly. 'Okay, I understand. Do I get to go now?'

'You get to sit and wait in here. I think one of your deputies is downstairs still. He seemed to be quite amorous with the girl on the reception, I'll send him up. He can undo everything, but just remember that if I don't get my wishes, then I'll be back for you. There's a phone number in this mobile,' said Dom setting one in front of the chief. 'When you find out the arrangements, you text them to that number. Do not call that number, otherwise it will not be answered, and I will come and look for you. I do not want to see you; I just want your message. If the message is not here within the next forty-eight hours, I will come and meet you as well. Like I said, next time will not be so pleasant.'

He heard Carrie-Anne snigger again, showing just how drunk she was.

'And don't shout when I leave the room, okay? If you do, like I said previously, I'll come and pay a visit.'

'Okay,' said the police chief. 'Just go, just get it done with.'

Dom walked out of the room with Carrie-Anne in tow. She half stumbled along behind him, and he put her in the elevator pressing for the ground floor. He went down the stairs, walked out from them and saw the police chief's assistant still talking to the girl at the front desk. He walked past and dropped the key into the man's pocket without him realising, before waiting outside for Carrie-Anne to stumble her way back out.

Once she was outside Dom called the hotel, advising the young girl in reception to tell the young man that his boss was upstairs waiting in the room for the key from his pocket, and that he needed to be released. With the call closed down, Dom walked with Carrie-Anne over until he found his car.

He didn't know if his plan had worked. He wasn't sure what he'd be going into, but for now, he'd done all he could, so he quietly drove the car back to the little hut in the middle of nowhere.

On arrival, Dom scouted around it, realised no one was there, opened up the door and flicked on the light. Kirsten was lying with a sheet around her on the sofa. Dom had seen Carrie-Anne had fallen asleep in the car and so he carried her out, placed her in his bed, and put blankets over her. He then locked up the house and sat in the darkness of the living room, watching Kirsten breathe slowly up and down.

He heard Carrie-Anne snoring from the other room. His mind was sitting and weighing up the options, wondering how quickly they could move and if they could, how far did he go and what did he do with his invite? Eventually, Dom fell asleep knowing he'd had a good evening, even if Carrie-Anne would wake up in the morning with a stinking hangover.

# Chapter 15

'He's been a changed man since we got out,' said Carrie-Anne to Kirsten as they stood looking at Dom outside the hut they were occupying. He was staring off at the sea in the distance, which still shone blue even though they were well inland. A small patch of it lay beyond two large hills but for Kirsten, it gave an image of serenity and peace during a time that there didn't seem to be much.

'Sorry to bring you into it again. I didn't know where else to go with Craig being . . .'

'Don't apologise,' said Carrie-Anne. 'If we'd come to you, you'd have done the same. You'd have jumped on a plane and got here. I can't operate the way I used to. In a stand-up fight I wouldn't be as much use these days. We have to operate a little bit cleverer. I really don't want to be back in amongst it.'

Kirsten looked over at a friend and colleague she always thought looked the model of a professional woman, but there were more trembles and jitters within Carrie-Anne these days. She looked more on edge, less riding the top of the wave and more getting carried along with it.

'If it hadn't been Craig, I don't think we'd have come. Certainly, wouldn't be coming back for any old mission.'

'You think this man will call?' asked Kirsten.

'Oh, he will. As sure as that headache I had this morning. I drank an awful lot to get him to come back to the room. At least Dom was there to threaten him properly. If I'd had a gun, I probably would've missed him, or worse, set it off accidentally before it even began.'

Kirsten grinned. It wasn't really funny but they were in that stage when you were waiting for something to happen, and you just fill the void with small talk because it took away the nervousness about what was ahead.

'Look,' said Carrie-Anne, 'there's the text.'

The pair watched Dom staring at his mobile phone. They could see him nodding a few times before the phone was put down and he turned and walked back at a steady pace towards the small hut. As he walked in through the door, the two women were already staring at him eagerly anticipating what he would say.

'It's on tonight. There's a small bar about five miles away. It's on the edge of a cliff down towards the coast, and we're both going to meet him there. He said no weapons once we go in.'

'I'll keep watch from a distance then to operate as a sniper,' said Kirsten.

'You're sure you're up to it?' asked Dom. 'It's a hell of a beating you took.'

Kirsten cocked her head towards him. 'Of course, I'm up to it. There's no option, Dom; you're not going in without cover. This is Craig we're talking about. If it wasn't, I wouldn't send you in.'

The man simply nodded and walked through to the kitchen. He could be heard putting coffee on. Kirsten looked to Carrie-

Anne, questioningly.

'He's not happy about it. He obviously doesn't think we've got good cover here. Have you brought any earpieces? Something so I can hear what's going on.'

'Of course, we have. Turn around a minute.' Kirsten turned her back to Carrie-Anne and the woman lifted up her top.

'It's starting to seep through again. I'll have to redo these bandages. Your back's never going to be the same. Do you realise that?'

'I'm not sure much of me is going to be the same after that,' said Kirsten, but she was resolute. When they'd first found her, she was a mess. Now she'd taken that mess, she'd shoved it to one side, and the tiger within her had come out.

'Dom, are we good?' she shouted through from the front room. Dom appeared at the edge, looking around from the kitchen, with a cup in his hand.

'Good as can be expected,' he said, 'but it won't be easy. Frankly, I think it's a trap.'

'Are you happy to go in though?' asked Kirsten.

'I don't see we have a choice. This is our only lead. Craig's time could be running out, but for the record, no, I think it's a trap.'

'Is there any other way to get someone else in there?'

'No,' said Dom. 'Carrie-Anne's got to come in with me. At least with two of us, we might have a chance if things go south.'

'But I'll keep the sniper rifle trained on the room, keep it outside as best you can.'

'I know how to do things,' said Dom. 'Don't worry about that. Just don't be too slow on the trigger.'

Dom slept for a large part of the rest of the afternoon, before later that evening, the three of them got in a car and drove towards the bar. They passed it several times before Dom dropped Kirsten off with a bag of weapons up on the hillside. In her black gear, she stalked her way up, positioning herself with a high advantage and a straight line down to where she saw the bar.

It had a path leading down to it and was cut into the side of the cliff, leaning out somewhat with a large drop off the edge of it down to a ravine below. The water from there ran straight out to the sea, less than one hundred metres away. The view from it must have been spectacular.

Kirsten was also pleased because they had an open veranda, plenty of room for her to get her shot in. She holed up and waited for night to fall and Dom and Carrie-Anne to make their move.

Scene break. Scene break. Scene break.

Dom parked the car and climbing out, he watched Carrie-Anne join him. She looked awkward these days, not the graceful woman of before. The damage she'd suffered from the attack by the Huntress had left such a mark that Dom knew she was never coming back. This was an extreme circumstance, one the pair of them had not been happy about, but when did you leave friends in trouble? Especially when it was their loved ones at stake.

Dom took Carrie-Anne's arm and escorted her down towards the bar at the edge of the cliff. The short track down was dusty. As they arrived, two men stepped out dressed in chinos and open shirts, with automatic weapons at their sides. There was no attempt to hide them. Clearly, this was a location you didn't wander into by accident. Carrie-Anne slipped out a gun from her hip and Dom took his from his jacket, placing them both on the ground before stepping forward. The two men raised their guns and escorted them down to the bar.

The lights of the bar were weak, but several candles lit the rest of it up. As Dom tried to look out to the hillside, he couldn't see anything in the darkness, one of the problems that being beside the brighter light caused. Other areas were even worse, his eyes unable to penetrate the darkness without significant light. A new customer was out there. A weapon would be trained on the men around them, but it was a lot of bodies for one person to take out if things went wrong.

One of the men pointed to a seat for Dom and another one for Carrie-Anne before walking to the bar and asking if they'd want whisky. Dom nodded. The two drinks were brought back, but Dom wasn't intent on touching his. He looked around, noted that no one seemed to be particularly in charge at the moment.

There was a car arriving in the distance. A few minutes later, a man walked down and into the bar. He gave a clip around the ear to one of the men standing there. He apparently had taken his gun off Dom. The man chastised him in Greek, and Dom understood just how brutal a chastising it was. The man then turned, walked over to Dom, and put out his hand.

'I'm the one you seek. You're looking for the man who was apprehended. Are you prepared to pay for him; other people are?'

'I am,' said Dom. 'I'm not happy he's been taken but I am prepared to pay so there's no more difficulties with the arrangement.'

'Other people are prepared to pay as well, other people who are not so bothered about his welfare, and better people to deal with. Who are you representing?' the man asked Dom.

'Myself and other people who have a deep interest. Let's say that this is the quiet way to do it.'

'Are you British?'

'I once was,' said Dom. It was always good not to lie too much, just in case somebody had found out something about you.

'We've been doing a bit of digging on you,' said the gangster. 'You did indeed work for the British, but you've retired as well, and now you're here. You know a lot of other people will pay for you. You've been very brave coming here as well,' said the man.

He walked over to the bar side looking down to the ravine below in the darkness. 'If we threw you over here, no one would know. Your body would be found down there at some point. More likely it would drop into the ravine and be washed off to the sea. I don't think you've come alone,' he said.

He reached up and pulled down the blind. The large piece of material covered up the view more than adequately. The man then instructed the others around him and suddenly the bar was enclosed, blinds down at the front and Dom realised that Kirsten wouldn't be able to see. She'd pack up. She'd run down, get close with her handgun, but she was a fair distance away, and had a ravine to deal with. Dom did not like the look of this.

The man stepped across to Carrie-Anne, ran his hand down the side of her face.

'You were highly spoken of as well when I talked to certain people. Certain people who would like the pair of you. I thank you for coming. We'll take you and we'll give you to the highest bidder. That's good business out here. Working with you would not be. It's nothing personal. I am fond of an older lady,' he said.

Dom felt that Carrie-Anne would certainly take that as an insult. He watched the man come closer to her and he knew she could sense that the situation had gone out of control. Her left hand had a slight twinge to it, one he recognised.

'I wonder who'll be the more valuable,' said Dom politely. It was a nothing statement, but the code word of valuable meant Carrie-Anne understood that the situation was now not about bargaining, but about getting out. As the gangster stepped closer to place a kiss on her cheek, Carrie-Anne grabbed him and bit hard into his neck.

The man screamed, but she was rising up with him, pushing him back as best as she could. He began to fall backwards, and she reached inside his jacket, pulling at the gun that he had. It came out, spilling to the ground and sliding on the floor and Dom made a dive for it. He picked it up as one of the other gangsters reacted, drawing a gun as well, but Dom was quicker, hitting the man straight between the eyes.

Another gangster went to react, but Carrie-Anne grabbed her drink off the table, throwing it at his face. She leapt down on the boss man. He turned around forcing her to the ground. At least he was between her and anyone trying to shoot, but the man was strong, trying to throttle her. Ten years ago, she would've been able to handle him, but the injury she suffered on the last days of her service meant she was weaker than she should be.

Dom went to help her, but he was struck across the back of the head and he fell to the floor. As he turned, somebody kicked him across the face, and he looked up to see a gun pointing down at him. There were at least four of them, all with weapons pointed. There was nothing he could do. If he retaliated, he'd be shot. All he could do was lie there.

He was almost in a panic. It had gone wrong. They needed Kirsten, but she'd still be travelling across. As Dom lay there, eyes wide in horror with the four guns pointing at him, he suddenly heard gunfire. The men fell suddenly, one after another in quick succession, and then a figure came across, kicking the man off Carrie-Anne. As the man got back to his feet, he charged the newcomer who put a gun up and shot the gangster as he ran at him. The man continued forward, grabbing the newcomer.

The newcomer spun on his heel, throwing the man away. He hit the edge of the bar area, his legs flying upwards. For a moment, he was caught in the blind. His body rolled, managed to extricate itself and tumble out from the bar down to the ravine.

Dom looked around. There was no one else there. Just the three of them, Dom, Carrie-Anne, and this new gunman. Dom noted that he had a hoodie on, his face unseen. Dom had clocked him coming in, but he had been sitting quietly in the corner.

'Drop the gun now.'

It was Kirsten, struggling for breath with her weapon pointing straight at the new figure. Hands were raised, and slowly the man lowered himself to the ground, placed the gun on the floor and then stood upright again. His hands went to his hoodie and slowly, he pulled it back, revealing who he was.

'I suggest we get out of here as quick as we can,' said Justin Chivers. 'A lot of noise, a lot of dead bodies, won't look good for any of us.'

# Chapter 16

Dom parked the car and watched Justin's car follow him around out of sight behind the hut. Together, four figures entered it and began to silently pack away their gear. Dom took a walk outside, checked that no one was following them, then came inside, closed up the hut as best he could, lighting two candles in the middle of it. The time was now past two in the morning, and they'd driven off in a rather random direction before coming to the hut just in case they were followed.

Justin Chivers had taken his own car, disappearing off on another track before meeting them at an agreed point and then routing to this hut. Dom made his way to the kitchen, put on the coffee, and everyone sat in silence until it was brought through, a cup placed in front of everyone.

Kirsten was sitting on a chair, Dom and Carrie-Anne on the sofa. Justin stood in one corner looking across at everyone.

'I don't mean to sound unwelcoming,' said Kirsten, 'but what the hell are you doing here? I wanted some background information. You weren't meant to turn up.'

'Oh, your thank-you is noted,' said Justin. 'I'm not here because of you. You called me and that afternoon I was bundled away down to Godfrey's cellar to answer questions about you, why you were in contact with me. Anna Hunt is also missing. Godfrey wants answers. That's why I'm here.'

'He sent you into the field? Why?' asked Dom.

Kirsten stood up, clearly in pain, stretching at her back.

'Is that the wounds again? Should we redo the bandages?' asked Carrie-Anne.

'Not now,' said Kirsten. 'Dom, you're not the only field agent. Justin can operate out in the field as well as anyone. Why do you think Anna had him so close? Where is she then?' asked Kirsten, turning to Justin. 'Do you know? Because I was with her not so long ago. She's not in a good way. They beat us and they . . .' Kirsten suddenly went silent.

'They did a lot more,' said Carrie-Anne, 'suffice to say.'

'Then we need to get her and get her quick,' retorted Justin.

'We need to get Craig,' snapped Kirsten.

'Okay, Kirsten,' said Justin. 'We need to get Craig; we need to get Anna. We need to get to the bottom of what's going on. I was here to reach out to you, find out what was going on. Godfrey wants you to work with him. He needs Anna back, you need Craig back, so that's why I'm here, but I know a lot more than that.

'Talking with our intelligence, the Russians are on site. It looks like it's time for payback. They feel Godfrey overstepped the mark when he blew up the Huntress, so they came for you all. Craig, you, and I imagine they'd have gone for Dom and Carrie-Anne eventually and possibly me, but we're not seen as their main targets. I didn't kill Control or her sister. Craig killed Control; Anna and you basically brought in the sister that Godfrey then killed. Godfrey's rather hard to get to, so I think they started off with his lieutenant, so to speak, but they'll go for him, too.'

'He's scared then, he wants to sort it. He wants us to go and sort it for him,' said Kirsten. 'Not happy. Not happy, Justin. I want Craig and I want out.'

'If we don't sort this, you won't be out. You get that?' asked Justin. 'It's going to be on your head.'

'Surely, Godfrey would've seen this coming,' said Dom. 'Surely, he would've . . .'

Justin put up his hands. 'It's why the Greeks are involved. Well, the Greek terrorists. They've basically been promised a lot, from what I can gather. That's the idea. Anna and Craig are being held by the Greeks to get the Russians' help to do something a little bit more dramatic than what they've done before. The mayor was a part of that. The ratcheting up of kidnapping tourists was because they knew you were here, knew you were about, but they didn't know exactly who you were. Bit of an amateur outfit and that's why it's got so messy. If we don't get to Anna soon, she'll be out of the country. From those on the periphery I've talked to, I know that handovers at the moment are a little bit dodgy. The Greeks are spooked. That, I guess, is due to you guys.'

'When they tried to trade Kirsten between themselves, myself and Carrie-Anne put a bullet in a number of them. We left the bodies there. We didn't tidy up. They probably think it was a terrorist-on-terrorist thing.'

'Who's got them then?' asked Kirsten. 'Tell me who's got them.'

'I don't know,' said Justin. 'One of the biggest problems we've got at the moment is the fact that everything is so fragmented amongst the terrorists. Imagine it's the same issue for our Russian friends. Otherwise, they would have identified who had Anna and Craig and got them out by now, but they're operating in somebody else's territory.'

Kirsten curved her back again. 'You need me to do those bandages?' asked Carrie-Anne.

'It can wait.'

'No, it can't. Sit down and I'll deal with it. You can continue talking.'

Carrie-Anne stood up, put a chair in the middle of the room, motioning Kirsten to sit down on it. She sat on it the wrong way round, her front facing the support of the chair. She let Carrie-Anne lift up her top clean off her. The men looked away respectfully as Carrie-Anne began to treat Kirsten's wounds.

'Who's got them?' asked Kirsten again. 'It's great to see you, Justin, like I said, but we really could do with a bit more help.'

'I can step in,' said Justin. 'I can get you all the help. I can link into our systems, but we are overseas here. I understand the bigger picture. We know that the Russians are looking for you, Craig, Anna, as a payback to Godfrey. Like I said before, the Russians are looking to be compensated for that. The mayor was the first thing. Our intelligence believes due to some of the items that the Russians have been acquiring, that they may carry out a terrorist attack here for the Greeks.'

'Have you told the Greek authorities that? Because to be quite honest, they haven't really bolstered the police force, have they?'

'We've told them, but the trouble is we can't tell them too much. Really want to tell the Greeks that all of this is kicking off because we blew up somebody else's agent?' said Justin. 'Not going to go down well internationally. We're telling them we've been getting rumours, tips, but there's not enough to convince them. That's why the police presence is so scant.

There's no army, nothing else. They also were going to panic away most of their tourists. This place lives off tourists, the money that they generate. I don't know if you realise, but Greece isn't that well off. The last thing it needs is to be known as a place you can't go to.'

'Why don't they come in now that terrorist attacks have happened?' asked Carrie-Anne.

'That's the other thing. I think there was meant to be a bolstering, but there's collusion going on underneath. Be very careful if you talk to Greek authorities,' said Justin. 'I got threatened the other night to not interfere. Of course, I gave the man a little bit of a thrashing just to explain my position, but it's not friendly territory out here at all whichever side you're looking at.'

'I don't care,' said Kirsten. 'What do we need to do? That was meant to be our link tonight, but all it was, was a trap. We don't know which terrorists have got Craig and Anna. How do we stop them?'

'We have to identify them,' said Justin, 'and we have to go at them.'

'What do you mean?'

'We go searching for them and we find out where their homes are. We pay a visit, put a little pressure on from our side. You realise we don't have to play this clean?' said Justin.

'Just hang on a minute,' said Dom. 'I'm operating here without any cover. I'm not like you on government business. You know I'm helping a friend, Carrie-Anne too. We were fat, dumb, and happy sitting enjoying our life. Now I'm okay to come back in and help, but let's set some ground rules about how far we go with things.'

'No,' said Kirsten, suddenly standing up off the chair. 'No,

Dom. We don't set ground rules. We have to get Craig back. Understand that's where I'm at. I thank you for being here, but that's the stand I'm working on, okay?'

Dom stood up as well and walked over to Kirsten. 'I need to know where we're going here. I don't want to be hunted for the rest of my days. Control didn't seem to be wanting us. Nobody came for us when we were in Austria. I'm truly sorry for Craig, but I've got a life to think of at the end of this. You might want to go no limits on this, but I'll have a life somewhere.'

Kirsten stared into the face of Dom, her face becoming angry. Then she felt Carrie-Anne stand up behind her, an arm went on each shoulder.

'Let's sit down and deal with those wounds again. Let's just chill out a bit. We're not at anybody's limit yet, so let's not fall out before it's even begun.'

Kirsten sat down and some more ointment was dabbed onto her back. She looked over at Dom who clearly wasn't happy.

'Kirsten's right though,' said Justin. 'There's also possibly going to be an attack if these Russians make a connection. It might also be the one thing that's preventing Anna from going anywhere. We need to get more information and we need to get it fast. We'll have a job tailing down the Russians. They're professionals, they're good. These Greek terrorists, amateurs in a lot of ways, started to punch above their weight. I say we go in, we find them, and we have a proper word with them.'

'I'm okay with that,' said Dom. 'That's why you go after them. Just be aware that I'm not one hundred percent with all of this, and I need to be.'

Kirsten nodded and the room fell silent. Only the occasional wince from Kirsten filled the thoughtful void.

'All done,' said Carrie-Anne. She handed back the top Kirsten had been wearing. She pulled it back on and then stood up in the middle of the room, looking at her three colleagues.

'In the morning, we get up and we identify the main leaders of the terrorists, we get a location for their home, we try and get a location for their business, and then we pay them a visit. It's important we stay together on this one, but I realise that you're out on a limb for me. Let's get a couple of hours sleep and let's get back at it, hunt these guys down, find out where they're keeping Anna and Craig, get a rescue together, get out.'

'What about the terrorist attack that might come from it?' asked Justin.

'Firstly,' said Kirsten, 'that's not my issue. My issue was always Craig. I'm happy to make Anna an issue as well. That's your issue, Justin, that you've been tasked in with.'

'I understand that,' said Justin. 'Godfrey won't. Once in the service always in the service, but I get that. Let's hope we can find out some details in the morning. By the way, where am I sleeping?'

Carrie-Anne stood up and walked through to one of the bedrooms before bringing a sheet back. 'Up, Dom,' she said. 'You're on Justin's bed.' Justin walked over as Carrie-Anne threw a sheet down on it and Dom stood up. He turned around as Justin got closer and put out his hand.

'Thank you,' said Dom. There was a brief handshake. Dom nodded and walked away before Carrie-Anne walked up to Justin and threw her arms around him.

'God bless you, Justin, God bless you.' She turned, popped a kiss on the cheek of Kirsten before walking off to the bedroom with Dom. Kirsten was left standing with Justin and her mind was racing.

'Anna said that Godfrey did it because the Huntress was too dangerous.'

'She probably was, but always a risk, always risk for the backfire that comes from it.'

'Well, let's see if we can outrun it,' said Kirsten, smiling at the operations man.

# Chapter 17

Waking up at six in the morning, Justin was keen to get to work, stationing his laptop in the middle of the lounge area of the hut, and by eight o'clock, he had come up with several locations for the various terrorist leaders. He had used the resources of Godfrey, highlighting who they thought were the main players, and then reducing the possible locations of where these people lived. By nine o'clock, the four of them were out on the road, Dom and Carrie-Anne in one car, Kirsten and Justin Chivers in the other.

As they toured the island looking at the various houses, Kirsten wondered what was going on. She'd had recent experience of tailing a gangster on the island, possibly involved with the terrorist side of things. She knew that they were busy generally running their own businesses, but every house they went to seemed to be quiet. As Kirsten stood up in the hills, binoculars trained across to another hill and the front door of one particular terrorist leader, she realised that she'd seen no movement at the house.

'That's not normal, is it?' she said to Justin. The man was standing outside the car, taking a drink in the hot sunshine, and Kirsten could see the sweat rolling down the back of his neck. He had a blue shirt on with a pair of chinos underneath and some light brown shoes and looked like a tourist, if a slightly older one. That was the intention, of course. Kirsten was beside him, pretending to be a younger daughter, rock t-shirt and black jeans despite the heat, she hadn't stepped from the car because she was sore.

The injuries from her torture were still grating at her. She wondered just how well she could move, and part of her wanted to go for a run just to see what the effect was, but there was too much to do. She'd struggled when sleeping the previous night, even though it was only four hours. Every time she rolled onto her back, she was in pain, with her shoulders constantly twitching. She wondered if she was re-opening the wounds on her back, wounds that Carrie-Anne had done so well to administer ointment to.

Justin Chivers picked up his binoculars and looked across at the house in question. 'You've really got to hand it to him, haven't you? There's the pool at the back, and I think the kids are there, but nobody's coming out the front; nobody's going in either. You can see a couple of people manning the gates, but nobody's come to say anything. It's not normal. You're right, Kirsten, it's not normal.'

'Not the daily life of being a gangster, is it?'

'Indeed,' said Justin, and he immediately reached for his pocket as his phone began to ring. Kirsten watched him put it up to his ear and he spoke quietly. It must have been Godfrey. Kirsten picked up her own phone and texted Dom. A message came back saying there was nothing, no movement at any of their locations. As she put the phone away, Justin had come over and was handing her the phone.

'Miss Stewart, I take it that Mr Chivers has been of use to

you,' said Godfrey.

'You could say that, but he knows on what terms. Have you got anything else for us?'

'Mr Chivers has just said that there's no movement. What we know is that the terrorist attack that the Russians are going to carry out may only be a few days away.'

'Based on what?'

'Wire intercepts. The Russians have asked for some extra equipment. Equipment that we can only see being used in some sort of terrorist attack. It's not their normal run-of-the-mill items. We haven't been able to trace where they're going to. In fact, we were very lucky to pick it up at all, but it's on its way, so you haven't got long, Miss Stewart.'

'We haven't got long,' said Kirsten. 'I thought we were on joint operations at the moment.'

'Indeed,' said Godfrey. 'Mr Chivers says that you saw Anna Hunt recently. How was she?'

'Well, if she's anything like me, she's not in a good way. We were tortured.'

'Physically, I take it?' said Godfrey.

'Certainly physically, but in other ways as well.'

There was a silence on the other end of the phone, a pause that was not normal from Godfrey. The man seemed to have a statement for everything, but Anna Hunt was a weak spot, Kristen thought. She had been his pick, maybe she was more than that to him. Was she a favourite child, or was there something there, something more that he wanted that had never come to fruition? The man was so guarded normally, and it was hard to pick up these moments, but Kirsten had realised that at these higher levels, they may pretend that sentiment didn't come into their work, but they operated like everyone else. Sure, they covered it up better, but when the genuine feelings were there, sometimes they got the better of people.

'She'll be well looked after once we get her,' said Godfrey. It was cold sounding, but the delay had given Kirsten the understanding. He had struggled to prepare the words. 'Do make sure you bring her home soon.'

'Along with Craig,' said Kirsten bitterly.

'Of course. Both of them, and if we can stop this attack on the way, all the better.'

'If we don't stop them, they're gone. Soon as they go out of this country, we'll never touch them, will we?'

'Of course not, and they will come for you.'

'You realise this is being done because of you.'

'Your take on the situation is your own,' said Godfrey. 'I couldn't possibly comment to someone outside the service about that.'

'You couldn't have made her disappear in a better way?' asked Kirsten.

'You may not understand the operational workings in a situation like that. You have to be sure, completely sure. It can't be left to chance.'

'Well, you were completely sure. Maybe you should have thought of the consequences before.'

'If you've nothing helpful to say, Miss Stewart, I suggest we terminate the call. I always told Anna there was too much feeling in you. You couldn't separate yourself and the job at times.'

'I think in this phone call, you haven't either,' said Kirsten. 'She was alive, take that as the starting point. How she feels about you after what we've just been through, I don't know.'

The line went dead and Kirsten handed the phone back to Justin Chivers. He'd been only a few feet away and heard the whole conversation.

'It's no wonder he got rid of you.'

'I chose to leave. I followed my conscience and left.'

'No, he got rid of you. That's the line they tout. Nobody leaves, not like that.'

'Dom retired; he didn't leave, and yet here he is back in it again,' said Kirsten. 'I don't think you ever leave this life. Do you?'

'Well, I sure hope so,' said Justin. 'I don't want to be seventy-five looking over my shoulder. I don't want to be fifty-five looking over my shoulder.'

He put the binoculars up to his eyes again, and after a few moments, gave a shake of his head. 'This is wrong. They've gone to ground. They are . . .'

'Holding onto their cards until the big play has to be made. Whoever has them has them. It might not be the same terrorists, but until they see what's been done for them by the Russians, they're not going to give anything up and they're not going to move about to even give us the vaguest clue of what's going on. Do you think they've been pulled into line after what's gone on recently?'

'That's possible,' said Justin. 'Maybe whoever is the overall head of the terrorists has brought them together. Maybe there is someone to stand up and lead. They do have a united cause that can help people, that can bring them closer. Definitely a possibility.'

'Let's take the car back, rendezvous with the others.'

Justin nodded while Kirsten sent Dom a text advising their return to their hut was the decision she'd made. It would take twenty minutes to get back to the hut.  Then Kirsten pondered the situation in her mind. It seemed they would have to stop this terrorist attack. If the attack didn't go through, the terrorists wouldn't give up their prize, and at least Craig and Anna would continue to be held by the terrorists.  It wasn't a pretty place to be, but it was better than being with the Russians.

The other plan was to find Craig and Anna, but with the leaders having gone to ground, that wasn't going to happen by simple surveillance. Kirsten looked at the countryside as it flew past her on the way back to the hut. The parched grass, the dusty side of the road, the occasional stone being lifted up by the wheels of the car, all these rushed past her eyes, but she saw none of them.

Inside a decision was forming, a decision that she was fighting.  Macleod wouldn't be happy with it, she thought. Macleod would say I've lost it. Macleod would say . . . She picked up the phone, began to dial a number and then stopped. *You can't bring him into this, Kirsten. You can't bring him in. He said you would know. He said you should make the decisions. You had the ability. You can't lay the weight of this on him.*

As the car pulled up in front of the hut, Kirsten continued to sit while Justin got out. As he reached the front door, he turned to her. 'You coming in?'

'Make the coffee,' she said.

'Are you all right?' asked Justin.

'Just make the damn coffee,' said Kirsten, much more loudly than she intended. Justin stared at her for a moment before entering the hut. Five minutes later, Kirsten could smell the coffee coming out. Along the dirt track up to the hut, a car was sending dust into the air. Less than a minute later, it had it pulled up in front of her. Carrie-Anne and Dom stepped out of it.

'All gone to ground?' said Dom.

Kirsten simply nodded. 'I'll see you inside,' she said. 'We'll talk there.' Dom walked off through the doors while Carrie-Anne stood watching Kirsten.

'I told you, we'll talk inside,' said Kirsten abruptly.

'That's a big decision.' Kirsten simply stared at Carrie-Anne.

'We'll talk inside.' It took Kirsten another five minutes before she entered the lounge, and saw Carrie-Anne and Dom sitting on the sofa, Justin standing up as usual.

'I don't want a debate about this. It seems to me that if they've all gone to ground, we're going to have to give these leaders a reason to talk to us. When I was watching today, they had their kids in the pool. We pick one. We pick one of the leaders with family, and we kidnap the kids. When we've got them, we ask for what we want.'

'No,' said Dom. 'That's a line. No.'

'There's no other way,' said Kirsten. 'There's no other way to be sure. We haven't got the time. The question is not doing this, it's who we target, who we think the leader is, who is calling the shots, who's put them back in their cages.'

Carrie-Anne stood up, her arms folded. 'What do you mean there's no point of debate? Of course, there's a debate. These are children. You're going after children. I don't mind what happens to these sods, I don't care what happens to these people who perpetrate the evil, but we don't take kids. No.'

'We'll not hurt them,' said Kirsten.

'Won't you?' Dom spat. 'This is a line you wouldn't have crossed.'

'They have Craig. He will die. A lot of our lines need crossed now.'

'They don't need crossed by me,' said Dom.

'She's right, though,' said Justin. 'This is the call. We need to find the leader, and we need to go after him where it hurts. He's gone after Kirsten where it hurts, gone after Godfrey where it hurts. This is the play; we just need the balls to play it.'

'No. You're not appealing to some sort of macho attitude here. This is morality. This is kids,' Dom retorted.

'This is Craig's life,' said Kirsten. 'Get onboard with it.'

'Dom,' said Carrie-Anne, 'outside for a word.' The pair marched quickly outside of the hut, closing the door behind them. Kirsten threw a glance at Justin, but he simply shook his shoulders.

'Who knows?' he said. 'Who knows what they'll think?'

Kirsten downed her coffee, stood up, and tried to twist. Her back hurt. She could feel as if the openings stretched further where the whip had cut into her. She was getting desperate, she knew that. She felt desperate, but things were desperate. There was no way they'd find the Russians, no way. This had to be the play. With everyone gone to ground, you had to hit them where it hurt.

Ten minutes later the door of the hut opened, and Carrie-Anne came in.

'He's not happy. I understand you want Craig back, you want Anna back, but this isn't right.'

'I know it's not right,' said Kirsten. 'It's what needs to be done.'

'It does need to be done,' said Justin quietly.

'I know,' said Carrie-Anne. 'If we don't, most likely we'll lose Craig and we'll lose Anna Hunt. Understand this. If we go into this, Dom and I take care of the kids, we look after them, and no way in hell are we shooting them.'

'Deal,' said Kirsten. 'Deal!'

Carrie-Anne nodded, walked back out of the hut to tell Dom. As she did so, Justin approached Kirsten. After making sure the door was shut, he whispered to her, 'You're okay with that?'

'Dom and Carrie-Anne can look after the kids. It's not a problem.'

Justin shook his head. 'No, the last bit, the bit about killing the kids if we don't get what we want.'

'She needs to believe that,' said Kirsten. 'As for me, I still don't know how far I would go.'

# Chapter 18

'Are you sure?' asked Kirsten. 'Is this definitely someone at the top?'

'We can't find the person at the very top, but this person is somewhere up there,' said Justin. 'I have the address. It's one that Dom and Carrie-Anne were watching previously. The best bet is that the kids still have to go to school. I'm not sure if we'll be able to take them when they're inside.'

'If they go to school, maybe they'll keep them home instead.'

'We'll see,' said Justin. 'Well, let's get out there and suss the ground first. I'll disappear off with Carrie-Anne, come back with a new vehicle or two. We don't want to be using these ones, running people off the road.'

'Good idea,' said Kirsten. 'I'll ride up with Dom.'

It was the following morning from the heated conversation and the group were feeling a little disjointed. Little had been said once the decision had been made, only Carrie-Anne reiterating several times that when the kids had been grabbed, it would be her and Dom looking after them. Kirsten was under no doubt that they wouldn't let any harm come to the kids, and she thought that was maybe a good thing because she wasn't quite sure how she would react if Craig's life was on the line.

The drive out to the house was a quiet one, Dom taking the wheel and barely looking at Kirsten. As soon as they arrived on the hillside looking down, a house that was set amongst many others, Dom began outlining the area.

'As you can see, we can't come in from the rear or from either side, it's a no go for any type of extraction. We'll have to wait for the kids to come out. The school day should be starting soon, possibly within the next couple of hours, so I think that will be our best time. Jump them as they're on the move. I wouldn't be surprised if they sent a convoy out with them, though.'

'I wouldn't be surprised if they don't come at all,' said Kirsten. 'We'll need to keep our options open about going in. By the looks of it, breaching from the rear will be the best option. Although I agree, it's not a very good one.'

'Not very good one?' queried Dom raising his eyebrows. 'Suicide is what I would call it. We need them to come out, however we make that happen.'

'Then the school run better happen,' said Kirsten. 'Otherwise, we'll have to go in all guns blazing.'

She saw Dom shake his head and knew he was right. That would be an act of desperation, but the trouble was Kirsten had no idea how long she had, how long before this terrorist act would be enacted by the Russians, and then the handover of Craig and Anna Hunt would happen.

Anna Hunt was an interesting conundrum to Kirsten at the moment. She'd picked Kirsten, she'd backed Kirsten, they'd fought together, and then Kirsten had gone against her. And after that, they'd been tortured together. There was a bond there in what they'd suffered, one that was proving to be quite strong, certainly in Kirsten's mind. It was true that Justin was willing to risk things to go get her, but Kirsten wasn't so sure about Dom and Carrie-Anne. Although they'd come to help, they certainly weren't up for a lot of what was about to happen. They needed to stay professional, which was ironic, since they weren't even in the service anymore.

It was less than an hour later when Justin and Carrie-Anne turned up with two different vehicles. One was a minibus, and the other a fast saloon-type car.

'Any trouble?' asked Kirsten.

'No, hopefully when things get moving, they won't even notice the stuff's gone,' said Justin.

Kirsten looked over at Carrie-Anne. 'Doesn't feel right operating on this side,' Carrie-Anne said. 'We have our own cars. Feels wrong taking them.'

'That's where we are at the moment,' said Kirsten, almost unfeelingly and got a look from Carrie-Anne.

'There's movement,' said Dom. 'If you're going to have a plan to do this, we need it quick.'

'Okay,' said Kirsten. 'Justin and I will go in the front. We'll take the minibus, and we'll run them off with it. You two come up from behind, ram them if necessary from the back. I'll slow them down from the front. Then, we get all the kids in the minibus, and we get ourselves back to the hut. Take a wide route before we return.'

'Why are you holding them there?' asked Dom.

'Where else we're going to store them? Keep them blind-folded until we get them in a room, keep that room tight.'

'It means somebody's going to have to look after,' said Carrie-Anne.

'I thought that's what you've volunteered for,' said Kirsten.

There was a scowl back from Carrie-Anne before Dom turned around.

'Get in the cars. There's a three-car convoy moving. As far as I can see, they've just put a couple of kids in the back.'

Suddenly, the air of hostility amongst the group was gone as business took over. Kirsten jumped into the van with Justin, letting him drive to the front, closely followed by Dom and Carrie-Anne. Justin put the foot down until he passed by the house of the leader they targeted. The minibus took up a position directly behind the convoy. Kirsten could see Dom weaving in and out behind the minibus, getting a confirming look at the vehicles.

'They're in the middle one. One at the front had about four hoods in it, same as the one at the back. Nobody with guns in the middle one as far as I could see but that doesn't mean they don't have them secreted somewhere.'

Kirsten had a map in front of her and checked where the road went. Judging from the map, it seemed to be heading for a village that was less than two miles away. The route had several sharp bends and corners. Kirsten thought it ideal to run some vehicles off the road.

'About three minutes up ahead,' said Kirsten. 'That's where we will make the initial move. If we get pushed off, take over and head to the front. There're a few drops we should be able to push cars into and they will probably incapacitate them. Just be careful with the middle vehicle.'

'You don't say,' replied Dom.

'Have you got me though?' asked Kirsten.

'Of course, just get it done.'

Kirsten sat back while Justin put the foot down on his car as he approached the winding stretch of road that went around the side of what weren't quite cliffs, but terrain that certainly had significantly steep runoffs. As the convoy slowed to turn around one of the corners, Justin increased his speed, driving into one of the cars ahead, hitting it full on the rear and not stopping until he driven it off the corner bend.

He pulled the handbrake, just managing to keep the minibus about on the road. Ahead of them, the cars sped off. Realising that something was happening ahead of him, Dom took his car inside of the minibus and raced on ahead. As it went around another corner, Dom managed to clip the rear of the second car, spinning it and bringing it to a halt. Up ahead, the front car stopped, and doors began to open. As it did so, Justin was just arriving onto the scene again with the temporarily delayed minibus.

Kirsten rolled down the window, leaned out, and began to fire as Justin raced past the stricken car with Dom's bumper hanging off the back of it, having smashed it hard. The windscreen blew out, but Kirsten didn't hesitate, firing back and she saw one man tumble.

Dom kept his foot down, drove straight into the car in front, sending several of the men diving for cover. Kirsten was still in the here and now because she kept her seatbelt on, but she pressed the clip to undo it. She was woozy as she stepped out of the van, but she began to count those ahead of her.

On the edge of the road, someone stood up, a gun in his hand. Kirsten was staggering now, trying to find herself again, but realising that her previous wounds from her torture were coming back to haunt her. She tried to lift her hand up to shoot, but pain wracked through her body, and she collapsed down on one side, her hip giving way. She watched, however, as the man with the gun was lifted off his feet and flopped to the ground. Dom came into view. He raced over kicking someone else in the head as they lay prostrate on the ground and then fired a shot off at someone else.

'Clear, let's move these kids,' he shouted.

'The minibus has stalled. Radiator or leaking engine. I'm not sure it's going to start,' shouted Justin Chivers. He looked over at Kirsten, who was hobbling forward. 'Get the kids in the car,' shouted Justin.

He ran over and helped Kirsten towards the car. From a blurry eye, she could see Carrie-Anne covering the children's heads with some cloth, then holding them down in the back seat. Justin let go, threw Kirsten into the back seat as well, slamming the door behind her before he joined Dom in the front.

Dom turned the ignition, reversed the car, and he could hear scraping, as the front bumper fell to the ground. Dom put the car into gear anyway and it started to scrape along the ground as cars from behind arrived on the scene. He sped off round two corners, before the car was pulled up and Kirsten watched as Justin got out and started kicking the front bumper hard. It must have fallen off for she watched him pick it up in his hands and fling it off the edge of the roadside before climbing back in.

Cars arrived behind them. Most looked like tourists, but Dom shouted as he saw someone in the distance suddenly get out. The person took her weapon, rolled down the window, and leaned out, firing high above the high end of the crowd. To hit someone amongst all these people would be difficult and they'd run the risk of killing someone they hadn't intended.

Dom got the car going again, but Kirsten looked behind them, and several cars weaved their way through.

'We need to get out of here and get lost soon,' she said. 'Two of them at least following us.' Dom acknowledged her, and the car was suddenly flung off onto a dusty track that wound up into the hill. Watching behind, Kirsten could see as their dust fell, two more cars were trailing.

'They followed us.,' she said. 'Definitely with us.'

Dom put his foot down, driving hard, throwing Kirsten about in the back, her ribs aching, and she heard screams in her ears from the children. Carrie-Anne held her grip on them.

'Do you know where this goes?' asked Kirsten.

'No,' said Dom, 'but we need to go somewhere.'

As they raced along, they saw a farmyard building on the left-hand side. The entrance to it seemed dark, but Dom did not let up, driving towards it.

'At least we'll have somewhere to shoot from,' he said, but Justin suddenly screamed to stop. Dom put his foot down on the brake.

'Quick,' said Kirsten. 'Spin it around. Get the car around the back of the building.'

Almost as if he intended it all along. Dom reversed the car round until it was out of sight around the back of the building.

'As soon as they go through here, they'll see us,' said Justin. 'There'll be nowhere to get out.'

'Just stay here and get ready to go,' said Kirsten. She opened the door and climbed out, ignoring the pain in her ribs. The door at the rear of the farmhouse building was loose and she opened it, stepping inside, and running through the shadows to the front of it, where it was wide open.

Dom had intended to come through here. Justin had seen just in time that a large tractor was inside. Kirsten stood on the edge of the building and made sure that the cars had seen her. Then she stepped inside and ran towards the back.

Both cars came racing in, the first one, ploughing straight into the tractor without seeing it, hidden in the darkness, after such bright sunshine outside. The second one followed it and didn't have time to stop as it rammed into the first one. Kirsten jumped into their own car after shutting the door, and Dom drove off as fast as he could. There was a race back down to the roadside, but on joining, Dom quickly found the next exit, took it and several more, before stopping in the middle of nowhere and looking down at his phone.

'You know where we are?' asked Justin.

'I'm just finding out. We'll limp back. We'll pick up the other cars.'

'No,' said Kirsten. 'Into the nearest village, we'll take some other car and by the time we get back and get the other ones, they won't know the new one's missing and we'll ditch it.'

Dom drove on down into the nearest village. It consisted of about twelve houses, but it was easy enough to steal a car and bring it out to the edge of the village and swap the kids over. There weren't many people about, and certainly none on the edge of the village.

They swapped up the driver for completeness, Carrie-Anne driving, everyone else keeping their heads down until they made their way by a circuitous route, to where they had left the original cars. Once there, they transferred the kids from inside their newly acquired car, which they pushed off a hillside into a copse of trees. Kirsten and Carrie-Anne then drove the cars back to the hut.

Carrie-Anne took the kids inside to the bedroom and once she'd put a mask on herself, she allowed them the freedom of having hoods taken off their head. Standing outside, Kirsten could hear them crying, could feel their fear as they asked Carrie-Anne where they were and was she going to hurt them. The woman was a professional, so, of course, she had no intentions, but she kept up the pretence.

After she'd spoken with them, she stepped outside of the bedroom, closed, and locked the door behind her before taking off her mask. Kirsten went to speak to Carrie-Anne, but all she did was shoot her a look and disappeared off to prepare the children some food.

'We make contact soon as,' Kirsten said to Justin. 'Get me the number.'

Justin nodded. 'It'll take me a moment to set up. Got to make sure they can't trace anything back.'

'Soon as,' said Kirsten. 'Soon as.'

# Chapter 19

Kirsten looked over at Justin Chivers and received a nod, indicating that the phone line was prepared. It was unlikely that the terrorists would be able to trace them anyway, but it was always good to be covered. She looked down at the piece of paper containing the number she should dial, rang it, and then awaited the other end of the line. Someone spoke in Greek, but Kirsten wasn't about to mess about in another language she barely understood.

'I have his children. He'll want to speak to me now.'

There was silence at the other end and then a little yelp and someone was running. Kirsten held the phone to her ear, aware that Dom was looking at her intently. She could see his uneasiness in what they'd done, but Craig was at the core of this. She needed to get him back, however it happened. She had no intentions of killing the kids or even causing them serious harm. In some ways, she was glad Dom was here because she didn't know how far she'd go if things spiralled out of control. How desperate would she get?

On the other end of the line, there were shouts. She heard someone angrily talking to someone and then the phone was passed as someone's hand went across the mouthpiece, causing

Kirsten to lift the phone away from her ear before bringing it back. Someone spoke quickly in Greek.

'If you don't speak English, I suggest you get someone who does because I'm only talking in one language.'

There was a brief pause and then someone spoke. 'If you don't return them immediately, I will . . .'

"You won't do anything,' said Kirsten, 'because you don't know where they are. You'll try and trace this phone call, but you won't be able to do it. You may be wondering why I have such a funny voice. That's because the voice is being manipulated, so you won't even know if I'm a man or a woman. The only thing you'll know is that I have the children. One second.'

She turned round and nodded to Dom, who stood up, walked over to one of the doors behind which Carrie-Anne had both children with their heads covered. They were brought forward, and Kirsten put the phone up to where their mouth should be underneath. They were told to speak. She allowed them about five words each before sending them back to the bedroom under Carrie-Anne's supervision.

'You're aware that I have them. I need to know where you're holding the man who was taken at the same time as the mayor was killed. I also want to know where Anna Hunt is.'

'You've got to be joking,' he said. 'First off, I don't know where that man is.'

'That's the wrong answer,' she said. 'You need to find out and you need to find out quickly. We have two children. You have two hours. After the first hour, one will die.'

'I don't know where he is,' said the man, calmly. 'Only the boss knows that. You'll have to speak to the boss. Clearly you don't know where the boss is or who the boss is because you've spoken to me.'

This was true, but Kirsten wasn't going to let the man take the upper hand. 'We know that an attack is going to take place as well. Where?'

The man on the other end began to laugh. 'This is the trouble,' he said. 'You're talking to the wrong one. I don't know. Only the boss knows that. You think we would just toss that information about amongst us? You've seen how divided we are, but the boss isn't. He has a small group of people at the top who might know what's going on. They have chosen not to share it with the likes of me and that's fine. I do as I'm asked.'

'But you need to find out,' said Kirsten. She could feel her hands beginning to sweat, become clammy around the phone. In the sweltering heat of the day, the hut was not a cool place to be, and they had it locked down so no sound would carry outside of it. She reached down for a sip of water before continuing.

'I don't think I'm making myself clear. You have two hours. After the first hour I will ring you. You will tell me what's going on. If you don't, one of the children will die and you'll have another hour before the next one will die. I suggest you get to it quickly.' Kirsten closed down the call.

'And we're clear,' said Justin, 'but I'm not liking it.'

'Not liking what?' asked Kirsten.

'He didn't even flinch. I mean, not a bit. There was no sign of worry, nothing in his voice.'

'Do you want me to go and take a look? See where he heads off to?' asked Dom.

'No,' said Kirsten. 'We've got the upper hand. He'll come back to us. He'll find out. He'll let us know. If you're seen around him, you could get grabbed. Once you're grabbed, the stakes change.'

'I'm good, though. I won't get grabbed.'

'It's an unnecessary risk. I'm not trying to get anybody hurt here. It's just things are escalating. We need to make sure they don't escalate too far.'

Dom shook his head, walked over towards the room where the children were being held and put on a mask before entering. Kirsten sat down on the sofa with Justin looking across at her.

'She was right about you; do you know that?' he said.

'Who?' asked Kirsten, but she knew the answer.

'Anna Hunt. She told me once that Godfrey reckoned that you didn't have what it was in you. But Anna said you just needed the right motivation. You'd do whatever it took when something truly mattered to you. You managed it when you stopped that train into London. That was impressive, and right now, you're like a cornered beast, but you're thinking, you're thinking shrewdly. You've even got Dom there to stop you from going over the top. I'm not sure if you will be able to, though. It will all change when going over the top's the only option left.'

'You think I'll have to kill these kids,' she said.

Justin shook his shoulders. 'I don't know,' he said, 'but where are we going to get to? We're going to come down on him and he's either going to tell you and we're laughing, or he's going to say nothing, and you're going to have to carry out your threat. Otherwise, we end up with nothing. As far as I see it, Craig means that much to you.'

'And Godfrey wouldn't mind if I did it as well, would he?'

'No,' said Justin. 'And yes, for the record, I obviously will try and carry out my orders, but I don't think that's going to come to that.'

'I was a police officer before this. Detective Constable,' said Kirsten. 'I worked with a man with a core of decency. A man who didn't always get it right, but he always looked to try and be on the side of right. I almost rang him the other day to see how he would sort this out. Did you know what he would tell me? He'd tell me to trust myself. Tell me that I knew what I was doing. I think that's what he used to have to tell himself.'

'Anna spoke with him,' said Justin. 'He didn't get flapped easily, she said.'

'She barely knows him,' said Kirsten disdainfully. 'If she did, she might be a better person for it.'

'Anna's something else,' said Justin. 'Just don't cross her.'

'Too late for that,' said Kirsten. They sat in silence until an hour had passed. Then Justin set up the phone call again. Kirsten's hands were sweating as she put the phone up to her ear, and she felt like taking herself and just plunging under a shower. The next couple of minutes would determine a lot.

'That's an hour,' said Kirsten as soon as the phone was picked up.

'That's exactly an hour,' said the man on the other end. It was the same person who had answered previously. 'And nothing has changed. I don't know anything,' he said.

'Then the child must die.'

'Kill them, then. Which one are you going to pick first?' Kirsten could hear screaming in the background. 'I mean it,' he said, 'Which one are you going to pick first? The boy or the girl?'

Kirsten hadn't even looked to see who the kids were. She didn't want to. As soon as you saw their faces you'd actually feel for them. You'd have to think about what you were doing.

She couldn't allow herself that luxury. 'Any particular one you'd like?' said Kirsten.

'Kill the boy first,' said the man. 'He's a pest. He has been a pain since he came into the house. He doesn't take any instruction. When he grows up, he'll be useless.'

Kirsten was confused. It seemed an awfully harsh thing to say about your own son.

'Okay,' said Kirsten. 'You want to listen on the line?'

'Indeed. Absolutely. If you tell me where you are, I'll come around and kill him myself.'

Kirsten looked over at Justin. The man's eyes had narrowed. It was clear he was deep in thought. Then he looked up at her and mouthed the words, 'Ask if he's the boy's father.'

'Are you the boy's father?' asked Kirsten.

'The only reason those children are in my house is because of their mother, but you know what? You can always find another woman. Kill them. Kill the pair of them. I lost two good men this morning because of you, and I'll find you for that. But as for these two, you can chuck them in the rubbish.'

Kirsten swallowed hard, realising the situation they were now in. On the other end of the phone was a screaming mother and she could hear her being slapped across the face and told to keep quiet.

'Don't worry about their mother. She'll come round or she'll be leaving this house. In fact, because she's put me in this situation, maybe I should solve that straight away. It'd be easier for you hearing her go down. Best thing then for the kids, isn't it? They don't have a mother.'

Kirsten could feel herself sweating as Dom returned to the room. She put her hand over the mouthpiece.

'What's up?' he said.

'He's not the kids' father. He's threatening to kill the mother now.'

Dom shook his head, then asked Kirsten for the phone. She was struggling, not knowing quite what to do, but Dom grabbed it quickly.

'The children will be dropped off in one of the villages near to a school. I won't say which one, but you can collect them from there. If any harm comes to them, we will visit. I watched you all day today, I watched them leave, and I'm a good shot. Pick them up, carry on.'

The man laughed. 'Purple towel yesterday at the swimming pool,' said Dom, and the laughter stopped on the other end of the phone. 'I'll be watching.' He put the phone down.

'Well, we're buggered, then,' said Dom, looking at Kirsten.

'No, we're not. We need to find another one, somebody else to go after. Justin, you need to get higher up this organisation. Another link, somehow. We need someone that someone actually loves.'

'We are talking about a lot of gangsters here. Might not be that easy, especially considering the time frame.'

'There's no police officer or anything? You can't get into the records of the police?' asked Kirsten.

'Of course, I can,' said Justin. 'But they're in Greek, and it'll take me a while to translate, and I'll need to try and find where I'm going.'

'Just get it done,' said Kirsten. 'We're running out of time.'

'What do we do?' said Dom. 'What's your move?'

'We haven't got a move unless Justin comes up with some-thing,' said Kirsten. 'This was a bad idea. Get Carrie-Anne, drop those kids off, make sure they're safe. Then come back here; we'll work out what we can do.'

Dom nodded and trotted off to the bedroom while Kirsten sat down. She saw the kids paraded past, hoods over their heads, and realised that she still hadn't seen them properly, except for when they were first grabbed. Her ribs ached; her back was sore. She wondered just how long she could keep going without needing a proper rest. She stood up, walked over to the kitchen, took out a bottle of water, and began to drink it. After a moment, she let the bottle slip off her lips and water cascaded across her face. She turned the bottle back upright before much could hit the floor, instead simply soaking her top.

'Are you okay?' asked Justin.

'No,' she said. 'I'm not. I'm frustrated, I'm angry, there's nowhere to go, and it's not that we're shutting something normal down. It's too tight. We need better surveillance; we need people everywhere.'

'We're not at home, though, we're working abroad. It's different, very different,' said Justin.

'I'm beginning to understand that,' said Kirsten, and she picked up the remainder of her water and stepped outside of the hut. The dust cloud from the departing Carrie-Anne and Dom had begun to settle, but everything just felt parched. *How do people ever do this?* she wondered. *How do people ever get on top of things in this heat?*

'You let me know the instant you find something,' said Kirsten.

'And I was going to keep it to myself all day. Of course, I will,' said Justin, and his face was held tight by the draw of the screen in front of him.

'This time, make it a good one, Justin. We need a good one this time; otherwise, we're not going to . . .' She didn't want to finish the sentence. The ramifications were far too horrible to contemplate.

# Chapter 20

'Justin, I need something. Time is up against us.'

Kirsten stood with her hands on her hips looking at him and she felt weary. Part of her wanted to go and lie down somewhere, go and just crawl under a rock and lie there for the next two weeks, but another part of her was scared, scared for Craig. If the Russians carried out a terrorist attack for the Zante terrorists, then Craig would be gone—Anna Hunt too. But Kirsten would be lying if she said that Anna was topmost of her thoughts. Everything was about Craig.

She was panicking, missing that calmness Craig had. They'd become close over the last two months, really close, and it was difficult to fight back the emotion, to keep the clear and detached head that she'd been taught in the service.

'Frankly,' said Justin, 'I know you're worried, you're worried sick, and you're panicked, but please go away. I'm going to work on it and I'll give you something when I have it. Standing there looking at me doesn't help. Go check on Dom and Carrie-Anne.'

After the earlier aborted attempt to extract information from one of the other terrorist leaders, Dom had seemed rather morbid at the possibility of finding someone else. Justin, however, was upbeat. Kirsten had told Dom and Carrie-Anne to stay at the hut rather than head back out to find more information. She wanted her troops to be ready in case they had to move quickly.

She walked to the kitchen, made a cup of coffee for herself and Justin, and simply placed the cup in front of him before walking off to the bedroom. She curled herself up on the bed, wrapping arms around her legs, choking back any tears that were coming. Then came a rap at the door.

Kirsten said nothing, and the door opened. Her blonde colleague sat down beside her. Carrie-Anne placed an arm around her.

'He's good,' she said, 'Justin's good. He'll find something. He must think he can. After all, he hasn't said anything to you, has he? He hasn't turned around and said plan for something else. That means he thinks he's going to find something.'

'They could be planning it right now though,' said Kirsten. 'He could find it, and the next thing you switch on the television and there you have it, the act's been done, something's been blown up, and Craig's gone.'

'True,' said Carrie-Anne, 'it could, but thinking like that isn't going to help. You need to be prepped up, you need to be in the correct frame of mind. We need to be armoured up and ready to go.'

'I'm glad you came,' said Kirsten, 'both of you. I know this hasn't been easy for you. I know I've gone past where Dom would normally go, where you would normally go, and look at you. You're not the way you used to be.'

'No, I'm not,' said Carrie-Anne, 'but you're family really, aren't you? I mean, you can't turn on your own family at this time. You can't reach out for other people. You have to reach for the family you had in the service; we're here, so dry those eyes. Get back up and get your plans going.'

Carrie-Anne put her arms around Kirsten, held her tight, almost in a motherly embrace. Kirsten couldn't remember her own mother's embrace. It was so long ago now.

There came a rap at the door, and Carrie-Anne sprang up before opening it to find Dom there.

'He says he's got something,' said Dom, 'a possibility.' Kirsten was up off the bed in a flash.

They huddled around Justin Chivers's computer in the middle of the lounge with Dom shaking his head.

'Where's this come from,' asked Dom, 'to be exact?'

'Well, Cortez is believed to be second in command. This has come from some intercepts being picked up by the service. However, one of the guys on the ground believes he has a love child. He got a policeman drunk last night and apparently, it's not widely known but it is known. The policeman received a bribe to silence him. The love child is now an older girl, about nineteen, and she's going to be playing at the club at a retirement party for an old chief of police. The only problem is it's going to be packed with half the police force,' he said.

'It's not a problem,' said Kirsten.

'That is a problem,' said Dom. 'You can't just waltz in front of all the police force, you know. We're going to have to be slick about this if we take it on.'

'If we take it on?' queried Kirsten. 'We're taking it on.'

'Then let's be smart about it,' said Carrie-Anne. The blonde woman looked strained, and she rubbed the back of her neck.

'Smart about it how?' asked Kirsten. 'We just waltz in and grab her.'

'No. Think about it,' said Carrie-Anne. 'We've got half the

police force there, centre of attention is the old chief. Terrorist activity in the area. Let's make them think we're making an example of him. We go in. We grab him, take him out. In the ensuing mess, somebody grabs her on the quiet and gets her out of there, and we leave the police chief behind, unable to extract him properly or something.'

'Good idea. She might not even be missed for a while,' said Dom. 'We can make the call.'

'How close is he to her?' Kirsten asked. 'If it's going to work, he's got to be afraid for her.'

'She's his pride and joy. Apparently, he can't speak about it. His wife is in the dark, and unlike our previous one, it appears that the poor guy's caught in a dilemma. He can't just exchange his wife as he likes her, too. Love's a bitch sometimes, isn't it?' smiled Justin.

'Dom, let's knuckle down, get kitted up. You say she's playing at this gig tonight. We need to scope it. Find out where it's at, what's happening, and if possible, get inside. We can map out where everything is. We've only got a couple of hours. What time's it start?'

'Eight o'clock tonight,' said Justin.

'Fine.'

Dom disappeared out the front door along with Carrie-Anne, but Kirsten sat with Justin as he tried to pull up records of the building it was going to be in. For the next two hours, Kirsten sat and planned. She was going to take the main risk. She thought it only fair that she and Justin should be at the front of the attempt to grab the police chief. It could go seriously wrong. There could be a lot of trigger-happy police officers in there. They might carry their guns as well. She'd need to make it a clean grab, a fast grab, one that people would not have time to react to, but also then be able to hold it, be able to keep the attention on her, so it couldn't be too low key. She'd have to be in their face.

It was about seven o'clock when the team assembled in the cars to drive the short distance to the small village where the event was taking place. Kirsten had plenty of ammunition in the cars, but she was going in relatively quietly. She didn't want to look like she was so over-stacked with equipment that she couldn't simply be a terrorist. She was happy to let her dark hair flow out the back, and if she covered her face with a balaclava, maybe they would think she was a local terrorist.

People said she had a Mediterranean look about her. She realised she was in Greece, but at least it was all south of Europe. If they saw her skin colour, they'd recognise she was from the north.

Justin Chivers, as usual, looked immaculate. The technical man put his balaclava on, and you recognised the stalwart that he was. With a balaclava on, the shirt half open, the medallion hanging down, he looked like some old geezer from these parts. Kirsten smiled at that. Dom and Carrie-Anne, however, looked very much like tourists, and that was the plan, for they would be outside for most of this, making a grab in the quickest of fashions.

The two cars reached the village in question, and Carrie-Anne and Dom disappeared round towards the back streets with the car being hidden away as best they could. Justin and Kirsten parked their car just a short distance away, for they would need it to get out of town and walked quietly in the shadows until they could see the front of the club where the party was taking place.

People were strolling in now, mostly men, a few women as

well, and in truth, it looked like a fairly civilized affair, mates coming out for a night out. Across the street from the club, Kirsten crouched in the shadows checking the weapons that were on her. 'Remember, you want to keep this controlled, calm. We get the girl out, we drop the boss off, and we get away.'

'If people start shooting,'

'We get out,' said Kirsten. 'We get out and we get out quick.' She had ten incendiaries on her that she would toss into the room afterwards in such a fashion that the place would go up, but no one should get hurt. They'd have time to get out. Another part of her thought she didn't care. She needed to get Craig, and that was all that mattered, so they needed this girl.

Kirsten donned her balaclava, looked for Justin who had his on as well, and took out her handgun. She walked quickly and deliberately across to the club where a bouncer on the front door went to speak to her. She held the gun up in front of his face, forced him to turn around, and marched him straight into the club. Behind her, Justin closed the doors.

There was music playing from a sound system, and Kirsten nodded to Justin as they entered the room. He pulled out the automatic machine gun, pointed it at a number of police officers who backed off. Some of the women with them started to scream, and Kirsten could see one of the men had wet himself at sight of the gun.

Justin made his way quickly around the room and pulled the plug on the sound system, the drum beats suddenly falling silent and the room going echoey quiet. On the stage, Kirsten could see several musicians. They hadn't started playing but were setting their equipment up. Now they were simply staring at her.

Kirsten didn't want to speak, but she looked around her, identified the police chief, and marched the bouncer straight to him. On arrival, she swapped the gun on the bouncer's head for that of the police chief and stood looking at everyone. Justin moved his way around towards the door, started herding everyone together, pointing the gun, insisting they move into the middle of the room. As the crowd started to gather, some sixty of them, Kirsten took the police chief through the middle of them, holding the gun to his head.

Maybe not speaking was actually more worrying. Maybe this was more frightening. Then she saw some of them begin to laugh. They thought it was a joke. Maybe she was some sort of dancing girl who would suddenly reveal herself as the night's entertainment and not this nefarious person she was acting as.

She made the police chief go down on his knees, put the gun onto his head, where she reached around behind her digging out the couple of incendiaries she had. She handed them to Justin who set them alight and threw them into the far corner. It was a good choice, thought Kirsten, the fire would spread there but their opportunity to get out was more than adequate.

Slowly, they backed to the door, the police chief telling everyone something in Greek. Kirsten thought it was to remain calm, something like that. She could see some agitated faces. Maybe they thought she was going to lock them in, but there was a back way out of the building surely as well. She took the police chief out through the front doors and found several people on the street who started to recoil quickly from Justin's gun.

It was all too calm, and they needed some confusion. Justin raised the automatic gun into the air and fired off shot after shot before pointing it down at the people on the street. There were screams and they started to run here, there, and everywhere while Kirsten dragged the police chief over the road and into the alleyway.

As she did so, she saw Dom running amok in the confusion of the street. Once in the alleyway, Kirsten hit the police chief across the back of the head with the handgun, knocking him out and dropping him to the floor. She took off her mask, as did Justin, ran to the end of the street, opening up the boot of the car, and throwing the weapons in. They closed it, got inside, and sat there for a moment.

They were about to start up the car when someone ran around the corner. Justin grabbed Kirsten, began to kiss her on the lips, held her in the embrace until the person ran past.

'Go,' she said. He started the car and drove away.

'Well, that was different. Never kissed a girl before.'

She began to laugh, but inside she was trembling. Had the plan worked? Where were Dom and Carrie-Anne? They'd be in the middle of doing their extraction. *We can't go back though.* Instead, they drove out to the hut, arriving in the dark without switching on any lights, and simply lighting a few candles once they got inside. It took an hour before a car pulled up outside.

Kirsten had a gun on her and was watching through a small peephole, but she recognised the approaching figures as those of Dom and Carrie-Anne. Someone else was pulled out of the car, in through the front door, and taken straight to one of the bedrooms. The girl was tied up and left on the bed still hooded while they stepped inside back to the lounge to report to Kirsten.

'Went smooth enough but plenty of police there after the gunshots. Had to skirt round a bit, but we didn't get detected.

Need to move on this now,' said Dom. 'She's agitated, properly agitated. I'm not sure, she may have some condition or something. Her breathing's not great, very stuttered at times, like she's struggling.'

'Okay,' said Kirsten. 'Carrie-Anne, go in. Mask up and go in and take that hood off her. Try and calm her down. Give her some water, whatever. I'll make the call.'

Carrie-Anne gave her a nod, disappeared off to do her work while Kirsten turned to Justin.

'Find out where he is, get patched into him. We have to make this call.'

Kirsten watched the man get to work and stood upright as he did so. She was finding it was better if her back was straight. When she sat down on the sofa, the wounds seemed to open up more. She thought about the girl in the bedroom, and it came back to her, hanging upside down, the beatings, the kickings. She just wanted to get Craig back more than ever now, more than ever.

# Chapter 21

'I found him,' said Justin. 'He made a phone call recently from a mobile he's got. He's not the cleverest when it comes to technology. He seems to be out on the road. He was talking to a woman about meeting.'

'Do you think he's going to be alone?' asked Kirsten. 'It's one thing to ring him. It's something else to actually step inside with him, threaten him properly.'

'Easy,' said Dom. 'Compromising yourself there. What if he's not alone? Suddenly you're caught. Suddenly we're back to square one. Everybody's running after you.'

'Whatever happens, I think we'll be on square one, Dom,' said Kirsten. Dom went to react, but Carrie-Anne was back in the room and took him off to one side.

'There's no need for that,' said Justin.

'Stop it. Just stop it, Justin. We need to get on with this. Where is he traveling?'

'Cortez is on the road. He's heading towards Zante. Looking at where he was saying he was going, it's quite probable he's disappearing there in a hurry. The phone call was made to a Carla Manuel. From what I can dig up on her records, single mother. Might be one of his fancy women.'

'Did you get any of the conversation?'

'They did back at base, and they said it sounded like he was quite agitated, seemed to be heading off to her in a hurry.'

'Things could be on the move, then,' said Carrie-Anne. 'Best intercept him rather than make a phone call. He's liable to just put it down, not be interested.'

Kirsten stormed out of the room, into the bedroom where a girl was sitting with her arms and legs tied, a hood still on her head. Kirsten looked at her. Did she have something on her that said it was hers, something she wouldn't leave? She looked at the girl's neck and saw a chain. Reaching forward, she pulled at the end of it and a locket came up. She turned it over and saw a description in Spanish on the back.

'In here,' she shouted, mentioning no names. Carrie-Anne walked in. 'Read that.'

'It says from your father. Well, it says your real father.'

Kirsten pulled the necklace hard, and the chain snapped. She held the locket in her hand.

'Time to go meet the real father,' she said. 'Keep her tied up. We'll let her go soon as we have the information, but until we do, we need to sit tight with her.'

Kirsten marched out of the room, leaving Carrie-Anne behind and heard a quivering girl in the background.

'Get me the route of that car,' said Kirsten.

'Could be going along the coast road in. That's probably the quickest. Here.' Justin pulled out a map. 'He's left here approximately, oh, ten minutes ago. Even if he was flooring it, he couldn't be past here. If you sit at this junction, you should pick him up. He'll be in a white saloon car.' Justin passed the registration. 'That's something he always does. Takes that car when he goes to see people who aren't to do with business.'

Kristen nodded. Having Justin around was like old times, just a wealth of information. 'Thank you,' she said before turning for the door, but Justin held up his hands.

'Don't thank me. Godfrey's the one supplying all this. I wouldn't get to give it to you if Godfrey didn't sanction it. It's him you need to thank.'

Kirsten looked back over at Justin. 'There's no way in hell I'll ever thank that man. If I don't get Craig back, I'll be coming for him.'

'I should go with you,' said Dom, 'you're too emotional.'

'Just be ready, Dom. If you find out the information, Justin, we'll make a move, but we need the information.' Kirsten slammed the door shut behind her.

Night had truly fallen and Kirsten flicked on the lights of the car as she drove out along the track to meet the main road. It took her ten minutes to reach the junction that Justin had spoken of. On the way, she felt her hands gripping tightly onto the wheel. If Cortez had decided to head out to Zante after everyone was being kept under wraps, it must have been for a reason. Something must be on the move. She could feel Craig slipping away from her grasp. If she didn't find out what was going on, if she didn't interrupt it, he could be gone from the country tonight.

As she parked up at the junction Justin had described, she found herself sweating. Yes, the night heat was more extreme than she was used to, but that wouldn't have bothered her. Instead, she felt the sweat was coming from fear, an agitation building up inside her. It took only ten minutes before a white car shot past and Kirsten followed it without any headlights on. She drove up close behind him, wondering if he could see her, but he gave no indication, neither increasing his speed nor taking a different route away from Zante.

As he came up to a narrow stretch of road, Kirsten put the foot down, raced her car up beside him and drove it into the side of his. He tried to spin with the wheel, but she'd done this before and soon he was run off the road, coming to a halt. As she saw him reach down into his glove compartment, she leapt from her car, gun pointing towards him. As the man came back up, he saw her standing, quite happily looking at him, knowing she had her prize.

'I hope you understand English,' she said, 'because you don't want to do that. You do that, you're dead. You kill me, she's dead.'

Kirsten held up the locket. Slowly she edged round, watching as the man stared, glaring at the necklace. She indicated for him to open the passenger door, which he did, but only after he placed his gun on the passenger seat. Kirsten reached in, flicked it out of the car and sat down beside him. 'Don't make any sudden moves. Don't say anything until I ask you a question, do you understand me?' The man nodded. 'How good is your English? Can you speak it?'

'Yes,' said the man. 'My English is fine.'

'Good. I take it you recognise the locket?'

'Yes,' he said, 'and if she's harmed, I'll . . .'

'Don't,' said Kirsten. 'You're not in the driving seat here. She's unharmed, completely unharmed and I have no wish to harm her, but someone has someone of mine and if I don't get him, then I'll hurt anyone who's standing in the way.'

The man looked up at her, his hands raised and gave a slow nod. 'What is it you need?' he said. 'I'm in a hurry myself.'

'I need to know where the attack's happening.' said Kirsten. 'I need to know what it is, and I need to know where.'

'That's why I'm on my way. I need to get a woman out of Zante. Zante is where it's going to be.'

'Good,' said Kirsten. 'Where?'

'They didn't tell us. There were three choices of target. They were paranoid, paranoid that we would inform on them, use it to curry favour, so we worked on three choices. One building is the local law court. It's quiet. No one there currently. Another one is the main nightclub, Fat Larry's. American nonsense. Apparently, there will be lots of people in there. Lots of tourists. It'll be very bad for the island administrators.'

'The last one?' said Kirsten.

'Law enforcement sports club. There will be people in there working, training, football matches happening. Sports, all different things. It's where a lot of officers will go to relax from the big city.'

'And you don't know which one it is?' asked Kirsten.

'No. As I said, they didn't tell us. They asked for three targets, we gave them. Since then, they've gone off to do it themselves. What I do know is, it's a bomb. They're going to detonate a bomb. Then afterwards, once it's gone off and everyone's starting to run in, they'll fire rockets in to cause as much devastation and panic as possible.'

'But your own citizens will be involved. Local people. Everything.'

'They said we had to be brutal, but they wouldn't listen to us. For years we've talked about separation. For years we've talked about this island as well as the rest of the islands, and they don't do anything. We do posters, we have marches, but now we'll make them pay.'

'Who are these Russians?'

The man shrugged his shoulders, looking at Kirsten as if

she was daft. 'They are Russians. You don't ask who they are. Probably working for Russian government, wanting to destabilise the EU. Who knows? We don't care. We're following our agenda. They simply wanted some people from us.'

'So, the people. Where are they?'

'Off with another part of our organisation. No one knows, but they'll bring them afterwards.'

'To where?' said Kirsten.

'I don't know. Maybe only one set of people know. They have them. The other people that know are the Russians because they're going to meet them there. The less people know, the more difficult it is to stop.'

'Too true,' said Kirsten. 'Too true.' She held the gun up at the man's head. 'Do you know anything else?' The man was beginning to sweat now as well. He looked down.

'No. I just need to get to Zante to get someone out.'

'You're not the only one that needs to get to Zante,' she said. 'I know you. I know your illegitimate daughter. I can find the rest of what family you have. If I don't get my man back, I'm coming for you. All of you,' said Kirsten.

She couldn't believe the anger in her voice. She struck him across the jaw with the butt of a gun. He looked back at her, wiping the blood from his nose.

'I believe you,' he said. 'I really do.'

Kirsten stepped out of the car to her own, but as she went to get into the driver's seat, she suddenly thought of something and she stepped around to the front of the man's car, shooting both tires. She then retired to the rear of it, shot both of those tires. He was incensed, thrashing the wheel, but she pointed her gun at him.

'Make too much noise and I'll make sure you're quiet.'

Kirsten jumped in the car and spun away from the roadside, driving towards Zante. She picked up her mobile as she drove, pressing the face of Justin Chivers and the call was connected through.

'Justin, take the girl, dump her somewhere good on the way to Zante. That's where we're going. There's a bomb that's been planted at either the law courts, Fat Larry's nightclub, or the law enforcement sports club. One of those three is going to be blown up, but no one knows which. Afterwards, they're going to fire rockets from a distance. Justin, whatever you do, you keep running satellite. There's no way three of us can scan this city from below. The ground's going to be hectic. You keep an eye on it from above, feeding in what's going on.'

'We're on our way,' he said, and closed down the call quickly. Kirsten drove into the night, now with the headlights of the car on, as she sped as fast as she could towards Zante. She'd arrive at approximately the same time as the rest of them, as she'd had to head back along the road slightly to pick the man up at the junction. Cortez would be raging, but she didn't care. All Kirsten cared about was they knew where they were going. They could get there; they could stop the bomb. Keep the Russians from maintaining their promise. She hoped then the Greeks wouldn't hand over Craig. She could also tail someone, try and find out where they were meeting if he was going to be exchanged tonight.

Inside, Kirsten shook. She felt the bile rising to her throat, panic setting in. If she hadn't had somewhere to go, she wasn't sure she could have coped with what was going on. She was bringing Dom and Carrie-Anne into a dangerous situation, a bomb, rockets afterwards. This was the Russians;

they wouldn't mess about.

Wasn't like the gangsters. It wasn't like these so-called Greek terrorists who didn't really know what they were doing, amateur in a lot of ways. But if the Russians planted a bomb, it would be a serious one, one that would do what it was intended to do. The rockets afterwards, there was no need for it, but it was intentional. The terrorists were showing a ruthlessness.

No doubt, the Russians would enjoy everything being stoked up for the Greeks, for Greece to be at war with itself. They never really had been, yet by getting what they wanted, the Russians would ensure another country began fighting a war that wasn't really there. All this on top of getting Craig. All this on top of getting Anna Hunt. All this and looking for Kirsten. All to get back at one man, Godfrey.

Kirsten swore if he'd have turned up just now, she'd put a bullet between his two eyes and she wouldn't stop shooting until he was no more. A part of her was disgusted at herself, but another part was desperate, so desperate that she'd take anything now to get Craig back. There was no cost too high.

# Chapter 22

The lights of Zante came up, shining brightly after the darkness of the countryside. There was a beat to the city. Tourists flocking here, there, and everywhere. Kirsten tried to concentrate on the road, while at the same time working her mobile phone, picking up images that Justin was sending down to her. She looked across. She saw three locations marked, knowing they were the ones that would be potential bomb sites. The coastline was close to where Fat Larry's nightclub was located, but the law enforcement sports club and the law courts were further into the town centre.

Kirsten sped past there first. There was no activity in the law courts. She wondered what the point would have been of blowing them up. If it was the Russians, they go for the maximum damage. Surely, the law courts would also be heavily guarded. Even at night, there'd be people there. The law enforcement sports club was another difficult target. You were talking about people in there who understood what it was to face some form of terrorism. Amongst them, there would be the keen-eyed people. After all, that's why you were employed.

The nightclub at Fat Larry's would be crazy. Filled to the

brim, no doubt, of sweaty, drunk customers dancing the night away, copulating, and whatever else they were doing with thunderously loud music. Kirsten knew which one she would be going for. As she passed the law courts, she called down the phone to Justin.

'I'm not seeing anything. Nothing at all in the law courts. What have you got?'

'The sports club is quiet. Normal comings and goings. There appears to be more people close to the nightclubs. Hang on,' said Justin.

Kirsten continued driving, heading towards the nightclub.

'Just coming across the police radios,' said Justin. 'They're saying there's an issue with the nightclub. I think they're saying there's a possible attack on it.'

Kirsten realised that having disabled Cortez's car, maybe he wanted to get his beloved out. Maybe he called it in anonymously. Kirsten pressed the accelerator, driving as hard as she could toward Fat Larry's.

'Dom, carry on,' she said. 'We need to get there. I'll head for the club. Look for the bomb. You two, check out the aerial points around the club. See if we can stop the rockets.'

There was an 'a-firm' from Dom. As Kirsten got closer to the area, she saw plenty of police cars suddenly setting up roadblocks. *I can't do this*, she thought, and pulled over to one side, now abandoning her car. She was dressed in black trousers. They were the ones she would use for creeping around, but here she was out in the middle of a crowd. The black t-shirt on top was wrung through with sweat, and she could feel the lacerations from the torture starting to weep again and grip hold of the shirt. *I don't look anything like a nightclubber*, she thought.

She ignored the way she was and just kept running on towards the nightclub. As she reached the police checkpoint, she realised there was a lot of people on the other side trying to come back out. The barriers were not fully placed, and there was a gap, which she ran for into the middle of a sea of people.

There were cries from Greek police officers, but she ignored them, continuing to run towards a large building beyond which she could see the moon shining on the sea. Sweat poured down her face. As Kirsten crossed the road and arrived towards the building, where security men were telling everyone to depart, she skirted the edge, looked for an emergency exit door at the rear, and ran inside. A man complained at her in Greek, but she put her hand up, shoving him to one side.

*You're going to plant a bomb*, she thought. *You're going to plant a bomb. Where do you put it?*

'Justin,' she shouted, 'have you got any footage today of the nightclub?'

'Yes,' he said. 'I can get that. That's not a problem. What do you need?'

'See what deliveries they've had today. Somebody has got to plant this bomb, or it's going to get delivered. Deliveries would be the easy way for it to have access to the building.'

'Do they serve food in that place?'

Kirsten looked around. 'I don't know. I'm only seeing a bar. I'm seeing several bars.'

The lights were on inside and the nightclub looked strange being fully lit up. Kirsten ran over to one of the long bars, placing her hands on it, swinging her legs up and over and landing on the bartending side. She dropped down, scanned along underneath the bar to see an array of glasses. She swept her hand in, many of them tumbling to the floor and crashing into a million pieces, but she kept up the pace. Scanning into the darkness underneath, she continued to look down the row of bottles but couldn't see anything untoward.

As she got up from behind the bar, a man ran over gesticulating to her to get a move on. She pushed him away, and he grabbed her arm. She delivered a thunderous kick into him, stronger than she thought she should have, but it flowed out of her in a rage that she was struggling to control.

'Just get out yourself,' she screamed at him, and ran over to another bar, jumping over it and began to look underneath. When she came back to the other side having discovered nothing, the man was lying on the floor.

She ran over to him, picked him up, putting his arm around her neck, and dragged him out to the front door where she simply deposited him, shouting over to a police officer. Running back inside, she heard Justin screaming at her down her earpiece.

'Several deliveries today. Most of it looks like food. Some drinks, but mainly food.'

'Where the hell is the kitchen?' screamed Kirsten. 'There must be a kitchen.'

She saw a staff-only exit from the main nightclub floor and ran over, pushing both doors wide open. She was in a corridor, and she opened each and every door down it, finding several offices, and a store for some of the more expensive drinks. It was going round in a circle looping her back towards the main dance floor. The corridor, blank, except for the occasional poster of some DJ or a rave. She burst through the double doors at the end of that corridor and realised she was in the kitchen.

'I got the kitchen,' she shouted and started looking over it while another voice came over their comms.

'One rocket down,' said Dom. 'Looks like they're coming in from high-rises around here. Continuing to search.'

Kirsten didn't even acknowledge Dom but instead began throwing bits of food and large cartons about.

'Specifically, Justin. Specifically, what was arriving?'

'They're some sort of fishmongers of some type,' he said. 'Prawns, that sort of thing. Frozen delivery.'

Kirsten looked around and saw a chill room at the back. She ran over, pulling open the door, with the flashing light above it, indicating that access was available. Stepping inside, she started pulling off boxes with prawns on the side, boxes of fish, throwing them onto the floor, tipping them out as quick as she could.

'No, what else?' she shouted.

'Olive oil. There's an olive oil delivery by the looks of it, or olives, or something of that sort.'

Kirsten ran back out of the chill area, with sweat still pouring off her, even though now she was feeling much cooler. She looked along under metal tables of stainless steel in the kitchen. She saw tomatoes, she saw lettuce, and then she saw some boxes of olive oil.

Kirsten ran over, pulled the first one aside, throwing it on the floor, and the contents poured out as she ripped it apart. She grabbed hold of another one, tipping it on its side, cutting it open with a large knife she got from the table above.

When she grabbed the third one and stuck the knife in, no oil came out. Slowly, she set the box upright and began to cut more carefully down with the knife. As she pried it open, she took out her phone and initiated the light, spotting inside what looked like a package. She recognised the timer and the connections into the C4 inside. Kirsten picked the bomb up carefully, turned to walk outside and found herself sliding across a floor of olive oil. She slid this way and that, not lifting her feet, but preferring to continue the slide. She went hard up against the door.

She kept one hand out holding the bomb away from her as she slipped down onto her bottom. Carefully, she got onto her knees and walked on her knees right across the kitchen until she was clear of the lake of fluid. She realised her feet were also covered, so she kicked off her shoes and ran with the bomb to the nearest exit she could find. As she opened the door, she was greeted by a cacophony of sirens and noise. She saw ambulance workers, policemen, firemen all around, and she screamed at them to get back. Orientating herself, she looked around and then saw some yachts.

*That must be the direction for the sea*, she thought. *Need to get this somewhere safe.*

Kirsten ran as hard as she could, ignoring the dusty road underneath her feet, the soles cutting up on the rough ground. As she sprinted along, a policeman moved in to intercept her, but she drove her left wrist up into the underside of his chin, knocking him clean off his feet. More officers ran towards her, but she saw the quay edge and the water beyond. Just as she thought she'd be able to outrun them to it, somebody tapped her legs. She sprawled forward flying along on her belly, the dusty road cutting into her legs.

Her back screamed at her, her front too, and the wounds from her torture felt that they were ripping apart all over again. She looked behind and saw the man who had taken her down was also sprawling on the ground. He must have given some sort of tap tackle, but his colleagues were on the way, drawing guns at her. She got up to her knees, with every last ounce of strength she had, took the bomb, and threw it almost Frisbee-like, off the edge of the quay, out into the water. She hoped there were no boats close by. There couldn't be. She heard the voices around her shouting, she thought indicating that she should lie on the ground and not move.

Then there was a sudden silence. Someone moved in to try and take her arms, handcuff her behind her back. As they went to do so, the bomb detonated. A shower of water flew into the air causing the officers to jump back. Kirsten took the chance to roll onto her back, reach up and grab the gun of the nearest police officer to her. She swatted him with her leg, kicking another in the midriff causing him to drop his gun, and then fall to the floor before another punch got the third one up on the chin. She grabbed the fourth one, pulling him as she ran, making sure he was in front of the other officers with their guns. She headed for the nearest door, which was another entrance into the nightclub.

'That's another one taken out,' said Carrie-Anne.

'Bomb is detonated safely,' shouted Kirsten. 'I'm inside the nightclub again. I need to get out.'

Suddenly, Dom swore. 'Get down, Kirsten,' he yelled. 'Get down. Rockets firing, rockets firing.'

Kirsten looked around. She had burst onto the main dance floor. Behind her, she heard police officers chasing. There was gunfire, something above her shattered, but she didn't have time to think about that. No time to think about anything or protecting anyone else. The nearest bar was on her right, only three feet away. She jumped over it, landed on her back, ignored the glass that cut her back and desperately rolled in underneath the bar.

There was a sudden cacophony of noise. It seemed to Kirsten that the ceiling fell in. Dust was everywhere, and she simply covered her head with her hands. The initial explosion was deafening, but then everything above her seemed to drop. Bottles smashed, glasses were shattered, and Kirsten covered herself as tightly as she could as she heard pieces of masonry continue to fall.

It was like the world was ending. There were cries of horror and pain. Those who had followed her in would have been left exposed to the ceiling coming down. She couldn't see anything, for the dust was everywhere, and suddenly lights were going out because they no longer existed. It took over two minutes for anything to settle. Then there were the sirens in the background.

'Kirsten,' shouted Dom, 'Kirsten.' There was no answer on the comms.

'What's happened? What's happening?' asked Justin.

Dom didn't speak. Instead, it was Carrie-Anne, slowly saying, 'They fired rockets into the building. The roof has collapsed. She was inside, Justin. She was inside.'

# Chapter 23

The sound of debris falling had reached a crescendo. Then a sudden stillness seemed to be all around her. From it emerged cries and shouts. Some, she thought, were coming from inside the building, people who had been crushed, injured. Others may not have been shouting at all, of course. From outside, there were yells, weeping. The sirens still filled the night.

Kirsten tried to orientate herself, think where she was. She'd got under the bar. There'd been the explosion, the roof hurtling down. She looked above her. Close to her was the top of the bar. It was a lot closer than when she'd first gone under. Twisting herself round, she saw the crack line where the bar counter had almost folded, but it had kept a tent shape above her, one that probably saved her life.

Her hearing was somewhat confused. Behind the cries and the sirens, there was a ringing, and when she tried to lift herself, move onto her knees, she felt unbalanced. There was another voice speaking. She thought it was calling her name.

'Kilo, report in. Kilo.' It was the old call sign. It was Justin, Justin Chivers. He must be . . . She reached down, took her phone from her pocket. The line was open. 'Justin?' she said.

'It's . . . it's . . .'

'Oh, thank God,' he said. 'Whereabouts are you in that building?'

'Under a bar,' she said. 'I think I'm under a bar. Hang on, I'll try and get out.'

'The place is surrounded with police. Be careful.'

'Shooter's on the move,' said Dom's voice suddenly. 'In pursuit.'

'Copy,' said Carrie-Anne. 'Following.'

She had to get up. She just had to get up. She'd prevented the bomb going off. Well, at least she'd prevented it from blowing the nightclub to smithereens, but they'd fired rockets in. Maybe people wouldn't realise it wasn't the bomb that did it. Maybe they'd think it was the bomb. Maybe they'd trade Craig.

*Craig*, she thought. *They'll trade Craig.* Kirsten forced herself to her knees, and realised she was still in her bare feet. There was broken glass across from her where the bar had crumbled down. She rolled out, careful to avoid the glass beside her before standing upright on the bar.

The roof above had come down and she could see flashing lights around her. The bar top that she'd crawled under had had a solid metal ridge running in an L-shape through it. This had bent, but the debris had fallen away from it, broken across it. Kirsten had picked probably the only place of safety in the entire room. As she stood up, she saw a police officer coming towards her.

Automatically, she went on the defensive. He spoke in Greek, but his actions were soothing. His hands reaching out in gentle fashion, he tried to support her, carry her out of the building, or at least what remained of it. There were cries around her.

She looked to her left and saw a man without a leg. She couldn't stop, for the officer half carried, half dragged her out of where the building had stood to deposit her on the street. He called for a medic and they came running.

The man quickly started scanning Kirsten, but she put her hand up, trying to tell him she was all right, but then she coughed. The dust when the ceiling had fallen down had been immense and she must have coughed some of it in. He found her some water, indicating she should swirl it around her mouth and spit it out. Kirsten did as instructed and sat back, holding up her hand to the man, who turned to look for his next casualty.

'I have a sighting,' said Dom. 'I have a sighting. I'll try and get hold of them.'

Kirsten's head swam. Dom had seen them. Dom was onto them, Carrie-Anne after him. Dom would stop them, catch them. He may even put them down. A panic rose in her. The bile in her throat climbed again. If he did that, Craig . . . she might not see him again. She needed to tail them, tail them to the rendezvous.

It had happened. At the end of the day, it had happened, in whatever respect. The Russians would be demanding their prisoners. She reached for her ear piece, and spoke hoarsely.

'Dom, no. Follow, just follow. Even if you catch them, if they're Russians, they won't fold. They'll not say anything. He'll be gone, Dom. He'll be gone. Follow, do not engage.'

'Understood,' came the simple one-word answer, but clearly, Dom was not in agreement with Kirsten's instruction. He didn't have to be, as long as he did what she said.

'Justin, get Dom's position. Get a tail on that man. I'll get in pursuit.'

Kirsten stood up, her feet feeling weak, her legs like they could go at any time.  She tottered along the street in her bare feet. People drifted past her, some with blood pouring from faces, some anxious, panicked, looking for their loved ones. Groups of people sat, dressed up for a night's clubbing, scantily clad or in sharp shirts, but with tears on their faces, shell-shocked. Kirsten tried to ignore them, tried to think how she could end this.

She rounded a corner, needing to get away from the crazy scenes that were going on before her. She had to get back to doing what she did. She must find transport.

At the end of the street in a small car park, she saw a motorbike. She began jogging down the street with a little bit of confidence, testing up her muscles. Her back was killing her; her sides were in agony; everything hurt, but she needed to go for Craig.

As she reached the bike, sweat was pouring off her, running down her forehead and beginning to sting her eyes. She threw herself astride it and looked for where the key would be to turn the bike on and began fiddling with the fixtures underneath. It didn't take her long before the bike was on the move, heading away from the current situation. A roadblock of police tried to stop her, told her not to be driving around like this, but she mounted the pavement, swerved past a couple of people, and roared into the night. She could hear the shouts of the officers behind her, but Kirsten didn't care. She took the road round to the edge of town and then stopped, picked up and tapped her earpiece.

'Where is he, Justin? Where is he?'

'Just tracking you. Okay. Head to the north. Head round to the north.'

'Where the hell's the north, Justin?'

'Straight ahead from where you've come. Keep going. That'll take you around. He's heading out for the main road, back into the country. Dom's on foot behind him.'

'What colour? What clothes? Description, Dom. Description.'

Kirsten realised that they'd got so frantic they'd dropped the code words. They were on an open line. Hell, it might be all right. It might not.

'Blue shirt, black jeans,' said Dom. 'Careful, he's armed.'

'Clocked him,' said a voice. It was Carrie-Anne.

'On my way,' said Kirsten, and the bike roared round the streets. She had to weave through traffic, most of it racing in to deal with the situation, ambulances, police, and firemen. There were also people desperate to get out wandering the streets, and it slowed her progress. But as she reached the edge of town and stopped the bike, she hoped she wouldn't be too late.

'Where is he?'

She could hear Dom puffing, blowing hard. 'Just got into a car,' he said. 'White saloon, last digits three-niner-two.'

'Going your way,' said Justin. 'Got a feed on him. Going your way. Damn it, lost the feed.'

Kirsten sat, hoping the car would go past. If it didn't, they'd have lost him, and then it'd be like searching for a needle in a haystack. Her feet were sore, one now on gravel ground supporting her and the bike, but she was ignoring the pain. The other foot was sitting up on the bike, the metal stirrup feeling awkward underneath the ball of it. She didn't care that it hurt.

Kirsten saw a white car go past and immediately jumped in

behind, but as she got up close, she realised the number plate was wrong and broke off into the driveway of a house. She spun the bike round, and sat waiting again.

'Has he passed me yet?'

'I have no idea,' said Justin. 'Trying to re-establish feed.'

'Doubt it,' said Dom. 'Any time, though.'

Black car, red car, then there was a blue one. They were traveling slowly because the convoy out of town was having difficulties. Green car, white car. Kirsten fired up the bike again and accelerated in, two cars behind. She swerved in and out, trying to glimpse the number plate. Once she'd correctly identified the numbers, she settled down and held her mic close to her mouth as she drove slowly along.

'Tag identified. He's two cars in front of me. Get a link, Justin.'

'Roger, wilco,' came the reply. Kirsten felt the wind blowing her hair back. Maybe it would take some of the dust out of it. There was a stickiness to it, even though she couldn't put her hand on her hair, having to maintain her position on the bike. What would happen now? How would they get out? How would they extract Craig when it came to it? They were on an island a terrorist attack had just taken place on. Everything would lock down. Things would get tough, hard to move about.

She needed to stop thinking like that. She needed to focus on the one task ahead. That was finding Craig. As they cleared the town limit and the countryside started to roll in with its darkness, various cars eventually broke off taking different routes, but the white car continued on along the coastline. Eventually, the cars in front of Kirsten moved out of the way, stopping off here and there. Kirsten let the white car round one corner before switching off her headlight. She continued to follow behind at a reasonable distance and in the dark. It forced her to keep her eyes wide open, tailing the lights of the car ahead, trying to memorise where it had gone.

'Following.'

It was Dom's voice. They must have got back to their car, now heading after her. She rounded one corner and saw the car pulling off down a small track. She took the bike, driving down behind, but saw the track only ran for less than half a mile, so she pulled in off the track, dumping the bike in amongst the grass.

The softness under her feet was a relief. She reached behind her, patting the gun that she still held on her. It was tucked inside her black trousers, and thankfully, when they'd pulled her from the wreckage, no one had inadvertently put their hand on it. It was small and powerful but well secreted. She took it out now, aware that she didn't know what was around the terrain.

Ahead of her, she saw the car headlights and they stopped, the doors opening and the interior light of the car coming on. The man got out and she heard him descending towards the beach. Kirsten circled wide, routing down to the beach, across a small river, but when she got close where the beach would've left her exposed, she hid down in the grass. She tapped the ear piece, turning down the volume as best she could.

'I have sight. He's just waiting, waiting by a beach. I think this is the extraction point.'

'It doesn't mean he's bringing Craig there. It might be his own extraction. Recommend you take him,' said Dom.

'Negative,' said Kirsten. If there was any chance Craig would be dropped off here, she was going to wait and take it.

'We'll be there in five,' said Dom.

'Don't come too close. Park off up on the road somewhere and route yourself in from there. They've still got to bring someone to meet him. I don't want cars in the way.'

'Of course,' said Dom, and yes, she'd just told him to suck eggs, but Kirsten didn't care. They couldn't blow this. This was it. This was the one opportunity to get Craig. Assuming, of course, she was right and that he was coming here.

# Chapter 24

Kirsten could feel the bile again, sickening inside as she waited. It was like this was the moment of her life. The waiting was always the worst bit. When she was in full flow, when she was there swinging from corner to corner, acting on instinct, on feeling, if she was to be more accurate, that was fine. That was something that just happened. But here and now, she had to wait to see if she'd made the right decision, a decision that could cost her Craig. The team would be here soon too, Dom encouraging her to just go out there and check that agent down. And he had a point. He had a very good point. That was the problem. This was a guess. This was a hope for the best.

Kirsten listened in the night. She thought she could hear a boat in the distance. This was nothing unusual around the island, of course. There were plenty of pleasure boats, people who enjoyed the water. Even at night, you could hear some of them, although they were nowhere near as prevalent.

It was suddenly drowned out by the arrival of a vehicle coming down the path. She saw the lights and the Russian who had been hiding stepped out on the beach, waving his hands at them. The lights were pointed out towards the sea as the vehicle finally stopped. Kirsten thought she saw two people emerging from the front. They then opened the side doors, where more people were coming out.

One of them was dragged in front of the lights of the van. Kirsten could see there was a hood over the person. This was it. This was the moment she'd been waiting for. She stepped out onto the beach, gun in hand and saw a Russian in the lights. It was the man who'd come from the town centre, the man she'd followed. Two seconds later he was lying on the ground, two direct shots to his temple.

Kirsten dived behind a rock as gunfire came back towards her. She tried to get up to shoot back, but the amount of covering fire was enormous. Someone had a machine gun. She glanced down to the rock, saw legs in the light, went to shoot and realised she couldn't identify the hostages from any of the Russians. She had to dive back in as more gunfire swept overhead. The sound of a boat coming was now prevalent, the engine getting closer and closer. She'd screwed this up. She'd made a mess of this. She was pinned down, unable to move when she should have gone in a lot closer; she should have . . .

More gunfire. Somebody else was shooting. She managed to roll out briefly from behind the rock, saw that those in front of the car had begun to shoot upwards. Kirsten got to her feet and ran. Someone was spinning round in front of the van. Something was pointed at her.

She fired straight at whoever was there, then zigzagged as she ran across the beach. She saw a pair of legs in the van light heading towards the water. Getting close to them, she threw herself, knocking the person to the ground. It was another woman, and she swore in Russian, turning Kirsten onto her back.

Kirsten reached up, two thumbs in the woman's throat, choking her violently. She managed to turn the woman onto her back, put a hand up to her head, and snap the woman's neck, ignoring her violent death throes.

Kirsten stood up, saw someone in front of the lights go to shoot her and then saw them fly backwards, hit by gunfire from elsewhere. Kirsten stepped out in the light, looking towards the sea. Because the beam had been so bright, her eyes were struggling to adjust, but there were figures there, figures that were now being hauled into the sea. She ran over, sand kicking up behind her, feeling the cool water as she splashed into it.

Someone hit her with the butt of a gun as she got close and she fell backwards. There was more gunfire, some from the beach. Somebody fired from the boat as well. Kirsten managed to roll up, saw two figures at the boat without hoods on and fired at them both. They fell backwards, but there were other figures there. How many had been in the van? She didn't know and she couldn't tell where everyone was now. The scene was chaos.

She heard cries as somebody else hit the ground. Kirsten was struck from behind by someone. She fell forward but rolled to one side as they tried to punch her. It was something she'd learned early on. When surprised, keep moving, don't give them the chance to react to you.

The man reached forward. Kirsten was now on one side, and she whipped her legs around, grabbing him by the neck, squeezing tight. She didn't have time to put him to sleep, to do some sort of a hold and she couldn't break a neck simply with her legs. Instead, she hauled herself up to him, punching him in the head three, four, five times before falling off, knowing he'd be at the very least unconscious.

The headlights of the van were shot out and suddenly the whole beach was in darkness. Kirsten was just across from the boat, which was preparing to depart, the engines starting to rev up.

'No,' she screamed and ran towards it, throwing herself, grabbing the edge of it. Someone stamped on her hands with hard, thick boots and she felt like one of her fingers must have been broken.

She couldn't hold on. Her face went down into the water, her hands followed, but even there she could hear the engine through the water, and she knew the boat was going. She got up on her knees, crying at it not to go. Someone beside her grabbed her shoulder, then reached down for her neck. Almost belligerently, she drove an elbow into the person's face, then turned around and punched him four times in the face. She turned back, screaming at the boat, but it was disappearing, the sound getting further and further away. He was gone. Surely that was Craig under the hood. Surely, he was gone.

Somebody entered the water beside her and she looked round to see a small rocket launcher.

'Don't worry. I've got it.'

It was Justin Chivers down on one knee, the launcher on his shoulder.

'No,' said Kirsten. 'You'll blow them to . . .'

The rocket launched, the bright light behind it seemingly propelling it forward. For two seconds Kirsten's life almost stood still as she traced the rocket out, hoping it would miss the boat. Justin was doing what he needed to do, but there was no way he could be sure he wouldn't kill everyone on it.

There was an explosion, a large amount of water flew up into the air and the boat could clearly be seen listing wildly, despite the darkness ahead.

'We're clear behind,' said Dom. 'We're clear behind.'

Kirsten ignored him and started running out. The water went up past her waist, then up to her neck and she began to swim.

'Don't,' said Dom. Above the lapping water around her face, she could hear him entering the water with her. Kirsten ignored him, put her head down and swam hard, kicking for all she was worth, dragging her body through the water until she thought she was somewhere near to where the boat had been.

She treaded water and looked around. In the darkness, it was difficult to see, shades of black popping up here and there. There was a trail of fire, a small amount of fuel burning on top of the sea, but it barely gave any decent light. Kirsten saw a shadow on the far side of her and she swam over, putting her hand on a body. She went to pull up the head, but there was nothing there. She checked the clothing and thought it to be one of the Russian figures that she'd seen on the beach. She couldn't be sure, but it wasn't Craig, the build was wrong. She turned again frantically, Dom now having arrived beside her.

'We'll need to go. They're going to come here.'

'They won't come for a while. They're too busy. Look around, Dom, look around. They've got to be here. Craig's got to be here.'

Kirsten began swimming around erratically again, looking here, there, and everywhere. Then she saw someone floating on the water. Their feet were up as if something was caught underneath them, buoying them up. She swam over realising there were bare legs. As she approached, she recognised them as female legs. Then she saw the beatings across the belly in the dark, the fire giving a light just strong enough to give the correct image.

She pulled back a hood that was lying over the face of the person and she knew who it would be. Anna Hunt. Her eyes were closed, but Kirsten began to cry. She didn't check if the woman was alive. Instead, she called to Dom, pushing her towards him, but he said he couldn't, said he had someone.

'Is it . . . ?' she cried back. 'Is it . . . ?'

'Just get her to shore. I'll get this person if necessary. We'll come back. I can't tell from here, it's too awkward.'

Kirsten was a good swimmer, and she was able to hook underneath Anna, taking her back bit by bit towards the shore. Several times, waves splashed over her face, but she was running on automatic pilot now. As she got closer, she felt another arm come in under Anna. Kirsten stood up, the water up around her shoulders and together with Carrie-Anne she dragged Anna Hunt out onto the beach. She watched Carrie-Anne drop down.

'I think she's alive,' she said. 'I think she's alive.'

Kirsten could see Justin speaking into his phone, but she couldn't register what he was saying. She looked back out at Dom. He was pulling a man up onto the beach. Kirsten saw one long leg, and then in the dark she thought part of the leg was missing. The other leg was missing too. There was no shoe. There was nothing. The hood was off and she saw Craig's face. Dom collapsed on the beach, dropping Craig as the tide washed up around him. Kirsten threw herself down on the ground, tapping Craig's face. He was unresponsive. She saw his legs. Well, the beginnings of them. She knelt, tears welling up inside her, fear taking over. *Was he alive? Was he alive?*

'Speak to me,' she yelled at him. 'Speak to me.' She slapped his face. There was a moan, but nothing more. 'We need to get out of here. We need to go,' said Kirsten desperately.

She looked around at Dom, but he was just flat on his back, exhausted. She turned to Carrie-Anne. The woman was working hard on Anna Hunt, doing chest compressions. Kirsten looked down at Craig. There was a bloody mess at the end of him and there were no feet. There were no shins. Justin came over. Ripping off his shirt, he began to tie a knot at the end of Craig's legs.

'We need to go. We've got to get out of here. He needs a hospital,' said Kirsten.

'It's on its way,' said Justin. 'It's on its way. Help me, help me. You've got to help me. Now focus,' he said.

Kirsten's head swam, but her hands went through the motions, and she kept talking to Craig, shouting at him. Then there were voices in the dark, Justin responding to them, and boots jumped from a boat that had just been beached. Kirsten was ushered into the rear of the boat. Craig was taken to another one. She was soaked through, cold starting to affect her despite the warmth of the night. She felt the jolt of the sea as the boats took off and she cried. Images of Craig, images of what she'd seen. She looked down at her hands. They were bloody. Bloody from tying tourniquets on his legs. She knelt forward, realised that Dom was beside her.

'We'll see,' he said. 'We'll see.'

He held her tight. Kirsten threw her arms around him as the boats continued to bounce hard over the sea.

# Chapter 25

Kirsten lay back on the bunk, her eyes looking at the ceiling, but her mind seeing so much else. When they'd come onto the ship, they'd taken him as fast as they could. She hadn't seen Craig then for what seemed like hours, and it possibly was. Carrie-Anne had taken her, showered her, cleaned her up and had left her in silent contemplation.

Justin had come, apologised to her, but it wasn't his fault. She knew that. If he hadn't done what he'd done, Craig would've been gone, and he'd been gone to a life of hell. Instead, he fought for his life on a small operating table in the depths of a military ship. They'd done what they could, they said, but there was nothing below the knees to save. But they'd saved him.

She'd gone in when he'd woken up the next morning. He was woozy. At first there were tears of celebration at seeing each other, but then she'd had to stand and watch him cry, cry at his own legs that weren't there, cry in incomprehension, and she held him.

The captain of the vessel had come down and explained that he couldn't just let her roam around the ship as much as he understood her problems. He'd attached someone to her, a female officer who had slept in the bunk below Kirsten. The woman had been fine, keeping to herself, and had even asked Kirsten if she needed something. Drink was brought, food when she needed it, but she felt like a kind of prisoner on the boat, one under house arrest. She'd been able to visit Dom and Carrie-Anne, and they'd all met in a mess hall to eat, accompanied by the captain who explained the situation on land.

Zante was in a mess. The government was calling it a terrorist attack. There was no mention of Russians. The captain, of course, fed through everything that Kirsten said to him, and she was quite happy to give the information. He said that the surgeon believed Craig would be all right, obviously without the use of the bottom half of his legs.

The vessel was currently continuing its course, one that had been promulgated previously and had routine exercises to do in a part of the Mediterranean. There was no way it was going to deviate off that course, for if it did, people would start linking it to the incident at the beach. The vehicle was still there. There'd been traces of gunfire. No doubt some locals had seen something.

As Kirsten lay trying to get the image of Craig's missing legs out of her head, the officer below tapped her gently on the shoulder.

'There's a guest coming to the boat, coming by helicopter in the next couple of minutes. You may want to see them. I believe it's someone to do with the Service. They didn't give me the name, but they're here to see the captain and Miss Hunt.'

Kirsten hadn't given thought to Anna Hunt since she'd got

back. The last she'd seen, Carrie-Anne was saving the woman's life. After all, she assumed she wasn't dead if she was about to meet whoever was coming in. The woman escorted Kirsten out through the canteen, up various stairs to the top of the ship. She had to wait in the corner, dressed now in ship fatigues so as not to look out of place. The helicopter came in and dropped off one solitary figure before it departed.

Kirsten felt like running at him. She felt like taking him and throwing him overboard into the sea never to come back again. From beside her, she saw Justin Chivers walk past, extending a hand out to Godfrey who had just arrived.

'Good job, Chivers, damn good job. I take it Anna's okay?'

Kirsten stepped forward, pushing off a hand from the officer assigned to her. 'And well done to you too, Miss Stewart.'

Kirsten pushed Justin to one side and spat in Godfrey's face. 'Worth it, was it? Worth it?'

She threw a punch, poleaxing the man, dropping him onto the deck. She went to go for him again, but Justin grabbed her under one arm, and the officer assigned to her was there as well.

'Don't,' said Justin. 'That's enough. That's enough.'

She looked across at Justin Chivers and saw a face that was compassionate, but firm. What was she going to do, kill the man? Of course not. She'd made her point. She spat once more, and then turned and walked off. She heard Justin helping Godfrey up before she was escorted back down to the mess hall with the officer assigned to her. When she got down there, Anna Hunt was sitting at a table in the corner.

'Godfrey's here for you. He'll be wanting to speak to you.'

'He will,' said Anna, 'but he'll talk to Justin first. It'll be an hour or two. Come and sit with me,' she said. 'It's been a rough one. It's been very rough.'

Kirsten looked over and then Anna Hunt, who seemed almost more contemplative than she ever could be gave a wry smile.

'You feel bitter towards him, don't you?' she said, and then looked at the officer beside Kirsten. 'You can leave her with me. Get us some coffees or something, please. It's all right. She won't go anywhere.'

The woman looked, gave a simple nod, and turned away for coffee. Kirsten realised that she never went out of sight of the women.

'You want to kill him, don't you?'

'That I do,' said Kirsten. 'That I do. Craig's . . .'

'I heard,' said Anna. 'I'm sorry. I was very fond of him, myself. He's good. I hope the pair of you can still make it work.'

'Last time I saw you, you weren't looking too good,' said Kirsten.

'I'm still not good.' She turned her back, lifted up her top and Kirsten saw lines across it. Lines that were deep, cut into her from a whip.

'We all look the same.' Anna turned and lifted the front up to show her tummy. The woman was a mess.

'Did they torture Craig as well?' Kirsten asked.

'No,' said Anna. 'By the time we got passed on to the right people, Craig had come in from a different route. They were so fractious, so broken up, the terrorist groups or whatever they are. They just hadn't a clue what each was doing.'

'So, we were just unlucky then, to get a sadistic bastard like that.'

'But you never broke, did you?' said Anna. 'You're made of tough stuff, and you got out.'

'I only got out because of Dom and Carrie-Anne. I was dead to rights, gun at my head when they took people out.'

'But you brought them in,' said Anna. 'You got to the end of this, you saw it through.' The two women sat in silence until the coffee returned.

'Do you regret it? Joining up?' asked Anna.

'Of course, I do,' said Kirsten. 'Look at me. I wanted someone to share a life with. If I hadn't . . .'

'If you hadn't been in it, you wouldn't have found him,' said Anna. 'It comes and it goes. It comes and it goes; you don't know what you're going to get. You don't know people either.'

Kirsten raised her head, staring at Anna. She traced the woman's hair, pushing it back away from her face, and she caught the brief tear coming out of an eye. 'You blame him, don't you?' said Kirsten. 'Like me, you blame him.'

'He put us all in trouble, and for what? Because he wanted to stop someone. He could have held her; he could have done something else. The moment you go in without a cool and calm head, the moment you make it personal, it comes back to bite you,' said Anna. 'And we all suffered. I never ever felt anger at you like I feel for Godfrey. I was pissed off when you turned around and you disobeyed your orders, but you were doing what you were. I got that, even though I didn't agree with it,' said Anna. 'Godfrey's not the person to do that. Godfrey let things get on top of him. He killed off someone in a way that would bring reprisals. He put us all at risk.'

'The two of you are often close,' said Kirsten. 'Were you ever . . . ?'

Anna looked at her and the tears that came down her face gave Kirsten the answer. 'Then I'm sorry,' said Kirsten. 'I'm sorry.'

'I don't want pity. I want to get up and get on, go off somewhere else. I guess Zante town's out, though.'

Anna sat waiting with Kirsten, neither talking until the time had passed and Anna was called to see Godfrey. Dom and Carrie-Anne came down to the mess hall and everyone sat in silence until Godfrey came back in.

He walked over to Dom, extended a hand, and Dom refused it. Kirsten saw Carrie-Anne's face and thought there was more going on in the analyst's head than Kirsten understood.

'Well, I will thank you all anyway. I'll let Anna debrief you and Justin. Given your initial reaction, Miss Stewart, I don't think you'll be talking to me anyway. You neither, Dominic.'

'Just go,' said Carrie-Anne. 'Don't stand around. Just go.'

'I am sorry for the injuries to Craig,' said Godfrey. Kirsten stood and stared without a word and watched him all the way until he left the mess hall.

'One day. One day I will . . .'

'No, you won't,' said Dom. 'Don't. You've got a life to get on with now. You've got to find where you want to be. What do you want to do? You need to put this behind you. Do not make an enemy of him.'

Kirsten could feel Carrie-Anne coming up to her. The woman wrapped her arms around her.

'Dom's right. None of us need him to be an enemy.'

Throwing off Carrie-Anne's embrace, Kirsten marched over to the stairs and with her keeper in tow, she clambered up to the top deck, out to watch the helicopter which Godfrey boarded disappear out towards the horizon. She felt her fists gripping tight. She felt the rage inside her.

'Don't,' said a voice in her ear. It was Dom. 'Don't. Promise me you won't.'

'It's a promise I can't keep, Dominic,' she said. 'I'm sorry.' She turned, kissed the man on the cheek. 'Thank you for everything, but I'm sorry. Some promises you can't keep.'

# Read on to discover the Patrick Smythe series!

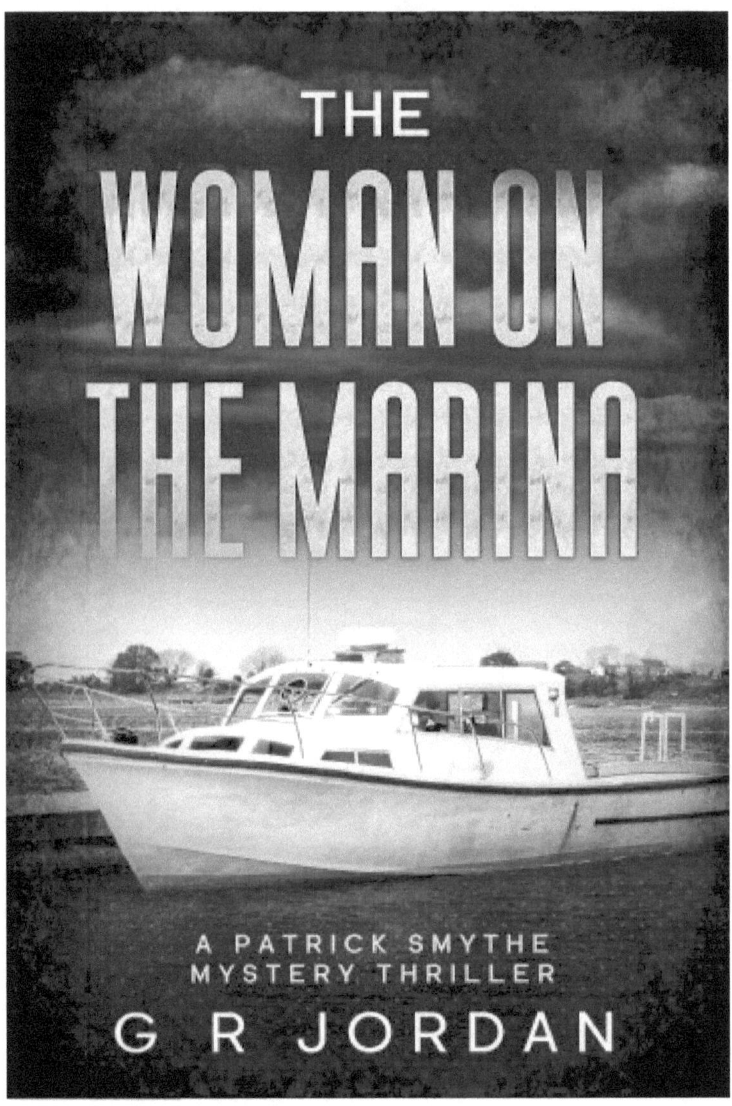


*Start your Patrick Smythe journey here!*

Patrick Smythe is a former Northern Irish policeman who

after suffering an amputation after a bomb blast, takes to the sea between the west coast of Scotland and his homeland to ply his trade as a private investigator. Join Paddy as he tries to work to his own ethics while knowing how to bend the rules he once enforced. Working from his beloved motorboat 'Craigantlet', Paddy decides to rescue a drug mule in this short story from the pen of G R Jordan.

Join G R Jordan's monthly newsletter about forthcoming releases and special writings for his tribe of avid readers and then receive your free Patrick Smythe short story.

Go to https://bit.ly/PatrickSmythe for your Patrick Smythe journey to start!

# About the Author

GR Jordan is a self-published author who finally decided at forty that in order to have an enjoyable lifestyle, his creative beast within would have to be unleashed. His books mirror that conflict in life where acts of decency contend with self-promotion, goodness stares in horror at evil, and kindness blindsides us when we at our worst. Corrupting our world with his parade of wondrous and horrific characters, he highlights everyday tensions with fresh eyes whilst taking his methodical, intelligent mainstays on a roller-coaster ride of dilemmas, all the while suffering the banter of their provocative sidekicks.

A graduate of Loughborough University where he masqueraded as a chemical engineer but ultimately played American football, Gary had worked at changing the shape of cereal flakes and pulled a pallet truck for a living. Watching vegetables freeze at -40'C was another career highlight and he was also one of the Scottish Highlands "blind" air traffic controllers.

These days he has graduated to answering a telephone to people in trouble before telephoning other people to sort it out.

Having flirted with most places in the UK, he is now based in the Isle of Lewis in Scotland where his free time is spent between raising a young family with his wife, writing, figuring out how to work a loom and caring for a small flock of chickens. Luckily, his writing is influenced by his varied work and life experience as the chickens have not been the poetical inspiration he had hoped for!

**You can connect with me on:**
🌐 https://grjordan.com
f https://facebook.com/carpetlessleprechaun

**Subscribe to my newsletter:**
✉ https://bit.ly/PatrickSmythe

# Also by G R Jordan

G R Jordan writes across multiple genres including crime, dark and action adventure fantasy, feel good fantasy, mystery thriller and horror fantasy. Below is a selection of his work. Whilst all books are available across online stores, signed copies are available at his personal shop.

**A Personal Favour (A Kirsten Stewart Thriller #9)**
**A friend's daughter goes missing when reporting for a local paper. A town on the up but with a history steeped in blood. Can Kirsten break the steely cocoon of silence and find the girl before she is another tragic story?**

Dealing with the desperate change in their circumstances, Craig receives a plea from an old friend to find his missing daughter. Being in no shape to assist, Kirsten takes his place and finds herself in a cold wilderness that lacks a warm welcome. When she digs too deep into the past, a desperate town seals itself off, leaving Kirsten trapped within.

*Some stories are just too personal for the public to hear!*

**The Death of Macleod - Inferno Book 1**
https://grjordan.com/product/the-death-of-macleod
**A slaughter of innocents. A crazed public demands vengeance from any source. Can Macleod hold his poise amidst a cry for blood before justice?**

When a heinous crime against children provokes a national outcry, Detective Inspector Macleod and his team are under pressure for results like never before. As the murders continue, top brass demands a scapegoat at all costs. But when Detective Sergeant McGrath suspects evidence has been planted to sate the public's bloodlust, can Macleod find the real killer before the public tears their sacrificial lamb apart?

*Today in the crucible, tomorrow the gallows.*

**The Disappearance of Russell Hadleigh (Patrick Smythe Book 1)**

https://grjordan.com/product/the-disappearance-of-russell-hadleigh

**A retired judge fails to meet his golf partner. His wife calls for help while running a fantasy play ring. When Russians start co-opting into a fairly-traded clothing brand, can Paddy untangle the strands before the bodies start littering the golf course?**

In his first full novel, Patrick Smythe, the single-armed former policeman, must infiltrate the golfing social scene to discover the fate of his client's husband. Assisted by a young starlet of the greens, Paddy tries to understand just who bears a grudge and who likes to play in the rough, culminating in a high stakes showdown where lives are hanging by the reaction of a moment. If you love pacey action, suspicious motives and devious characters, then Paddy Smythe operates amongst your kind of people.

Love is a matter of taste but money always demands more of its suitor.